A Discovery of New Worlds

D0800704

A Discovery of New Worlds

Bernard de Fontenelle

Translated by Aphra Behn

Published by Hesperus Press Limited
28 Mortimer Street, London W1W 7RD
www.hesperuspress.com

A Discovery of New Worlds first published in 1686

This translation by Aphra Behn first published in 1688

This edition first published by Hesperus Press, 2012

Foreword © Paul Murdin, 2012

Designed and typeset by Fraser Muggeridge studio
Printed in Jordan by Jordan National Press

ISBN: 978-1-84391-366-5

CONTENTS

FOREWORD

Bernard de Fontenelle's book of 1686, in this edition called *A Discovery of New Worlds* but with its original title translatable as *Conversations on the question whether there are other worlds*, is an early example of what is now a successful genre, a popular book on astronomy. But it has a distinctive seventeenth-century feature. It is written in the form of conversations that take place over five nights between a young teacher, Fontenelle himself, writing in the first person as a 'philosopher', and a titled lady, an anonymous Marquise. The couple flirt as they stroll under the starry evening sky through the parklands of the Marquise's country estate near Paris, but the body of the work consists of astronomical explanations about the Universe by Fontenelle, responding to comments and questions by the Marquise, which move on the flow of the philosopher's line of thought through the dialogue. This novel-like structure may have been one of the attractions of the book for its translator, Aphra Behn, one of the first English women authors and playwrights, and one of the main writers of 'amatory fiction', the chick-lit of the late seventeenth and early eighteenth centuries.

Fontenelle's Universe was driven by a force of gravity in the form envisaged by the French philosopher René Descartes, in his book *The World*, written in 1633. Descartes envisaged that around the Sun and each planet there exists a vortex in space, and that bodies that fall into a vortex are swirled around in an orbit. The term that Fontenelle uses for a vortex is *un tourbillon*, the French word for whirlpool or cyclone, translated and spelt as 'tourbillion' by Aphra Behn. In either form, tourbillon or tourbillion, the word is now obsolete in English (except as a highly specialized word for a twirly mechanism used in very expensive clockwork watches) but it is obviously related etymologically to words like 'turbulence'.

Fontenelle was writing a year or two before Isaac Newton put forward his theory of gravity (his major work, the *Principia*, was published in 1687), so he could not have considered Newton's theory. In any case, Descartes' theory survived in a senior conservative faction of the French scientific community for a long time after Newton's theory had taken hold in the rest of the scientific world, even though more progressive, younger eighteenth-century French scientists, such as Pierre-Louis Maupertuis and Alexis-Claude Clairaut, adopted Newtonian physics at an early stage. They were aided in its promulgation in France by the writer Voltaire, who saw it as an exemplar of the rational analysis to which the Enlightenment aspired.

According to Descartes' Vortex Theory, the space between the planets or between the stars may be empty of matter but vortices still exist as features of space itself. For example, in the conversation of the Fifth Night, Fontenelle uses the idea that empty vortices extend out into space beyond the Solar System to explain how the Sun sweeps up comets from interstellar space. What astronomers believe now is quite close to this, in that comets have their origin in the zone at the boundary between the Solar System and interstellar space, a region called the Oort Cloud.

The Vortex Theory addressed the philosophical problem that Newton swept aside in the *Principia* by the torrent of successful mathematical physics undammed by his theory of gravitation, namely the way that the force of gravity acts across empty space as 'action at a distance'. Descartes conceived of gravity as being transmitted from one body to another by the succession of vortices that lie between. Newton described what gravity does, while Descartes asked what gravity was, a question still unanswered satisfactorily. Descartes' question foresaw the modern basis both of General Relativity (which sees gravity as being transmitted by waves in the space between bodies) and Quantum Mechanics (which sees the forces between elementary particles as taking place by the exchange of other particles called bosons), namely that there is something that transmits the force of gravity across space from one body to another. So although Descartes' theory was mathematically useless, it remains philosophically interesting.

Fontenelle's book is known now primarily for its main argument that the Universe is filled with planets that are inhabited. The argument follows a modern form and boils down to the following: stars are suns, like our Sun, and, even if we cannot see them because the stars are so distant, they have planetary systems, like our Solar System. Those planets will be inhabited, like the Earth. Fontenelle's argument relies on what has become known as the Principle of Mediocrity, 'We should assume ourselves to be typical of any class we belong to, unless there is some evidence to the contrary.'

This argument that Fontenelle published in 1686 had been current for 2,000 years or more before, and it is still current more than 300 years later, although it is possible now to add considerably more detail, and some certainty to parts of the argument. For example, we know for sure that stars are indeed suns and the planets of the Solar System are worlds more or less like the Earth. We know of further planets (and similar worlds) in our Solar System beyond those known to Fontenelle, and we know that some of them are indeed very earth-like. We know even about planets that orbit around about 3,000 of the nearer stars. Most of them are big planets, since detecting smaller, earth-like planets is at the limits of our technology, but, extrapolating the evidence, some astronomers estimate that as high a proportion as a third of the stars in our Galaxy may have an earth-like planet.

Although we have no conclusive evidence that there is any kind of life on any of these planets (apart from the Earth itself), most scientists come to a similar conclusion to Fontenelle. They regard life as a natural phenomenon that came about as a result of universally applicable scientific principles on material that is similar to terrestrial material on the many planets that are earth-like. Putting the science in its simplest form, biochemistry and evolution operate on common chemical elements in the environments of those planets with a surface, liquid water and sources of energy like sunlight and volcanism – and produce life.

In the fourth century BC, the Greek philosopher Epicurus made an argument similar to Fontenelle's, not quite so specifically focused:

> There are infinite worlds both like and unlike this world of ours. For the atoms being infinite in number, as was already proved, are borne on far out into space. For those atoms which are of such a nature that a world could be created by them or made by them, have not been used up in one world or in a limited number of worlds... So that there nowhere exists an obstacle to the infinite number of worlds.

In this argument Epicurus was followed by his pupil Democritus, and the populariser of his work, the Roman poet Lucretius. But his argument was opposed by his contemporary, the philosopher Aristotle:

There must be only one centre [to the Universe]; and given this latter fact, it follows from the same evidence and by the same compulsion, that the world must be unique. There cannot be several worlds.

Aristotle did not accept the Principle of Mediocrity. He thought that celestial matter and terrestrial matter were fundamentally different, being made of different elements. Terrestrial matter was made of a mixture of earth, fire, water and air, while celestial matter was made of fifth element, 'ether', or 'quintessence'. It was the nature of quintessence to remain in the celestial regions, while the other four elements naturally gravitated to the ground, or near to it. It was impossible for quintessence to take up the properties common on the Earth, so the Earth was unique, and all that it contained, such as human beings, could not exist elsewhere. The planets were not worlds like the Earth, they were distinct celestial bodies that orbited around the Earth, and since they were made of material that was completely different from terrestrial material they were in no way like the Earth, and in particular not inhabited.

Aristotle's cosmology was taken up and given mathematical form in respect of the motions of the celestial bodies by a succession of astronomers, culminating with the Hellenic-Roman-Egyptian astronomer Claudius Ptolomaeus. He represented the Universe as a series of seven concentric crystal spheres carrying the Moon and the Sun, five planets (as we would call them now, namely Mercury, Venus, Mars, Jupiter and Saturn) and, circumscribing the planets, a crystal sphere containing the stars. The celestial bodies move eternally around the Earth with unchanging circular motion. There is just one centre to the rotating Universe.

When Europe became Christianised, Hellenistic astronomical theories were adapted to Christian thought. A link between what Aristotle thought and Biblical writings was forged in the thirteenth century by intellectuals at the University of Paris. They were known as Thomists, because they were led by the Dominican friar Thomas Aquinas. There was a chain of being that stretched from our changeable world up to the eternal celestial bodies, which became progressively more perfect the further away they were from the Earth. All the planets moved in perfect circles. The lowest planet, the Moon, was a perfect sphere but it changed its shape and had grey patches (the features known in folklore as the Man in the Moon). The Sun was thought to be spotless. The planets, from Mercury, Venus, Mars and Jupiter to Saturn, moved progressively more slowly, indicating a progressive approach to eternal lack of change. Beyond the celestial spheres, it was thought, lay the completely motionless, utterly perfect, unchanging, eternal dwelling place of God: heaven.

This world picture is one in which God's attention is focused on mankind as the unique pinnacle of His Creation and it guaranteed continued theological interest in the question addressed by Fontenelle of whether other worlds existed and were inhabited. The issue, with its theological aspects, became a prominent battleground between science and Christianity, to such an extent that it could be briefly referred to in the phrase 'plurality of worlds', as used as the original French title of his book by Fontenelle, without further explanation. It is remarkable that Fontenelle, educated at a Jesuit college, says nothing about any of the religious aspects but his omission was compensated by his translator Aphra Behn, in a preface that devoted many pages to scriptural analysis intended to resolve astronomical conflicts between the Bible and science.

Aristotle's world picture, elaborated by the Thomists, held sway for centuries but fell with the scientific investigation of the orbits of the planets around the Earth. These orbits were not perfect circles after all, but complicated hierarchical orbits of circles whose centres themselves moved in circles; such a system was called 'epicyclic'. After each improvement of the theory, however, the planets departed from predictions. To 'save the phenomena' and more accurately describe the motions of the planets the epicyclic system was elaborated but, however complex it was made, it proved to be inadequate. Searching for a system that would be more accurate, the Polish cleric, Nicholas Copernicus, in 1543, published his theory that the Sun was the centre of the Solar System. The planets orbited the Sun, including our world. This implied that our world was not unique, since it was a planet like others, although Copernicus never explicitly stated this. As a result, the Principle of Mediocrity is also called the Copernican Principle, after Copernicus' theory.

The Italian monk, Giordano Bruno took up the logic of the Copernican theory, suggesting that the Sun was a star. True it was brighter by far than the other stars, but that was because the Sun was so much closer than the nearest stars, as Fontenelle describes in the conversation on the Fifth Night. There could be innumerable stars that stretched off into the distant Universe, each with planets like ours. In 1591 Bruno put forward his ideas in a book *De l'infinito universo e mondi* (On the infinite Universe and its worlds). Bruno's views on Christianity, including his opinions on the number of worlds in the Universe, were deemed heresies, but he refused to recant and in 1600 he was burnt at the stake by the Inquisition in the Campo de' Fiori, Rome.

Copernicus' and Bruno's ideas were developed by the astronomer Johannes Kepler late in the sixteenth and early seventeenth centuries. First, he realised that the planetary orbits were not at all circular, they were elliptical, and less than perfect in the Aristotelian sense. Furthermore, he became convinced that the Moon, the Sun, the planets and even perhaps the stars were worlds like ours and might be inhabited. He went on to speculate about the nature of the inhabitants of the Moon, suggesting that they would live in shady caves, because of the effect of the heat of the Sun during the Moon's two-week-long 'day'. Fontenelle runs with a similar idea about the putative inhabitants of the Moon in the conversation on the Third Night.

When Galileo Galilei turned his telescope to the sky in 1610, he saw that the Moon was a rough sphere, with mountains and valleys, like the Earth and not distinctly different from it, as recounted by Fontenelle on the Second Night. Galileo saw that the planet Jupiter had four moons that orbited around it (Fourth Night), so there were in fact at least two centres of rotation in the Universe, not just the one, as Aristotle had thought. He saw spots on the Sun – it was not perfect. The present explanation is that the surface of the Sun is hot and gaseous and the spots are cooler depressions, active areas associated with arches and jets of gaseous material that look, as Fontenelle describes (Fourth Night), like erupting volcanoes.

Like Bruno, Gallileo was tried by the Inquisition for putting forward his views 'contrary to scripture' but he recanted and was punished less severely than Bruno, placed under house arrest for the rest of his life. However, although some refused to look through the telescope and see what they did not want to see, direct observation of other worlds had in reality settled the argument as to whether other worlds existed.

In his book, Fontenelle could describe little of the nature of the planets of the Solar System, usually just their size and how hot or cold they were (based on their distance from the Sun), but, in the century after Fontenelle, with telescopes of greater power, astronomers were able to investigate their environmental properties. To the modern reader, Fontenelle's most startling statement on the Fourth Night about the planets is that Mars 'contains nothing rare or curious that I know of… in short, Mars is not worthy the pains of a longer discourse'. His opinion was based on the science of the time, and it was not until 1781 that in Britain William Herschel could articulate the growing realisation that Mars had a 'considerable but moderate atmosphere, so that its inhabitants probably enjoy a situation in many respects similar to ours'. Now Mars is seen as one of the most likely places in the Solar System where there may be life beyond Earth; for this reason Mars is the main target of twenty-first-century space exploration.

Although science has confirmed that planets are ubiquitous, and most people still make the same argument as Fontenelle that they may have life on them, some scientists question whether extraterrestrial life is intelligent, like us, or even as complex as terrestrial animal life of any kind. There were some lucky flukes in the history of our Earth that have given our planet properties extraordinarily favourable for intelligent life, such as stability for long enough for it to develop. For example, by chance there was a massive collision between the embryonic Earth and another small planet early in the history of the Solar System. This gave the Earth not only the Moon but also a large iron core that has maintained a strong terrestrial magnetic field that has defended our atmosphere and the life it nourishes from destruction by solar particles generated by those disturbances characterized by Fontenelle as 'solar volcanoes'. Without some accidents like this, it is argued, life would not have developed the complexity that we now see. This is supported by the observation that simple unicellular life (like bacteria, or the similar newly identified family of creatures called archaeons, a name that implies that they are viewed as the earliest forms of life) developed on Earth quickly after it formed (in the first ten per cent of its history), whereas complex multi-cellular life – eventually, animals – developed only recently (in the last ten per cent).

In this view, the present constitution of life on Earth is rare. The flaw in the Principle of Mediocrity may be that it took human beings to formulate it and that fact in itself may guarantee that, although our planet and bacterial life may be mediocre, life like us may not be. There are probably many, many planets like ours, and some of them have life on them. But not many will have life like ours. There is a plurality of worlds, but not many have inhabitants with whom, as in this book, you can have an intelligent conversation.

– Paul Murdin, 2012

A Discovery of New Worlds

TO MONSIEUR DE L ——

Sir,

You expect I should give you an exact account in what manner I passed my time in the country, at the castle of Madam the Marquise of —— but I am afraid this account will enlarge itself to a volume, and that which is worse to a volume of philosophy, while you, perhaps, expect to hear of feasting, parties at play and hunting matches. O, Sir; you will hear of nothing but planets, worlds and tourbillions, nor has there been any other things discoursed on. Perhaps you are a philosopher, and will not believe my discourse, so ridiculous as it may appear to the less learned; and possibly, you will be glad to hear that I have drawn Madam the Marquise into our party. We could not have made an advantage more considerable, since I always esteemed youth and beauty as things of great value. If wisdom herself would appear to mankind, with a design to be well received, she would not do ill to assume the form and resemblance of Madam the Marquise; and could she be so agreeable in her conversation, I assure you, all the world would run after her precepts. You must not expect to hear wonders, when I shall make you a relation of the discourse I had with this beautiful lady; and I ought to have as much wit as herself, to repeat all she said in the same graceful manner she expressed it; however, I hope to make you sensible of the readiness of her genius, in comprehending all things; for my part, I esteem her perfectly witty, since she is so with the most facility in the world. Perhaps you will be apt to say, that her sex must needs be wanting in those perfections which adorn ours, because they do not read so much. But what signifies the reading of so many vast volumes over, since there are a great many men who have made that the business of their whole lives, to whom, if I durst, I would scarce allow the knowledge of anything? As for the rest, you will be obliged to me. I know, before I begin to open the conversation I had with Madam the Marquise, I ought, of course, to describe to you the castle, whither she was retired, to pass the autumn. People are apt, on such occasions, to make very large descriptions, but I'll be more favourable to you. Let it suffice, that when I arrived there, I found no company, which I was very glad of. The two first days there passed nothing remarkable, but our time was spent in discoursing of the news of Paris, from whence I came. After this, passed those entertainments which, in the sequel, I will impart to you. I will divide our discourse therefore into nights, because, indeed, we had none, but in the nights.

THE FIRST NIGHT

We went one evening after supper to walk in the park; the air was cool and refreshing, which made us sufficient amends for the excessive heat of the day, and of which I find I shall be obliged to make you a description, which I cannot well avoid, the fineness of it leading me so necessarily to it.

The Moon was about an hour high, which shining through the boughs of the trees, made a most agreeable mixture, and chequered the paths beneath with a most resplendent white upon the green, which appeared to be black by that light. There was no cloud to be seen that could hide from us, or obscure the smallest of the stars, which looked all like pure polished gold, whose lustre was extremely heightened by the deep azure field on which they were placed. These pleasant objects set me athinking, and had it not been for Madam la Marquise, I might have continued longer in that silent contemplation; but the presence of a person of her wit and beauty hindered me from giving up my thoughts entirely to the Moon and stars. 'Do not you believe, Madam,' said I, 'that the clearness of this night exceeds the glory of the brightest day?'

'I confess,' said she, 'the day must yield to such a night; the day which resembles a fair beauty, which though more sparkling, is not so charming as one of a brown complexion, who is a true emblem of the night.'

'You are very generous, Madam,' said I, 'to give the advantage to the brown, you who are so admirably fair yourself. Yet without dispute, day is the most beautiful thing in nature; and most of the heroines in romances, which are modelled after the most perfect idea fancy can represent by the most ingenious of mankind, are generally described to be fair.'

'But,' said she, 'beauty is insipid, if it want the pleasure and power of charming; and you must acknowledge that the brightest day that ever you saw could never have engaged you in so agreeable an ecstasy, as you were just now like to have fallen into by the powerful attractions of this night.'

'I agree to what you say, Madam,' said I, 'but I must own at the same time, that a beauty of your complexion would give me another sort of transport than the finest night with all the advantages obscurity can give it.'

'Though that were true,' said she, 'I should not be satisfied; since those fair beauties that so resemble the day, produce not those soft effects of the other. How come it, that lovers who are the best judges of what is pleasing and touching, do always address themselves to the night, in all their songs and elegies?'

I told her that they most certainly paid their acknowledgments to the night; for she was ever most favourable to all their designs.

'But, Sir,' replied the Marquise, 'she receives also all their complaints, as a true confidant of all their intrigues; from whence proceeds that?'

'The silence and gloom of the night,' said I, 'inspires the restless sigher with thoughts very passionate and languishing, which the busier day diverts a thousand little ways (though one would think the night should charm all things to repose) and though the day affords solitudes and recess, groves and grottoes, equally obscure and silent as the night itself; yet we fancy that the stars move with a more silent motion than the Sun, and that all the objects which the heavens represent to our view, are softer, and stay our sight more easily; and flattering ourselves that we are the only persons at that time awake, we are vain enough to give a loose to a thousand thoughts extravagant and easing. Besides, the scene of the universe by daylight appears too uniform, we beholding but one great luminary in an arched vault of azure, of a vast extent, while all the stars appear confusedly dispersed, and disposed as it were by chance in a thousand different figures, which assists our roving fancies to fall agreeably into silent thoughts.'

'Sir,' replied Madam la Marquise, 'I have always felt those effects of night you tell me of, I love the stars, and could be heartily angry with the Sun for taking them from my sight.'

'Ah,' cried I, 'I cannot forgive his taking from me the sight of all those worlds that are there.'

'Worlds,' said she, 'what worlds?'

And looking earnestly upon me, asked me again, what I meant?

'I ask your pardon, madam,' said I, 'I was insensibly led to this fond discovery of my weakness.'

'What weakness?' said she, more earnestly than before.

'Alas,' said I, 'I am sorry that I must confess I have imagined to myself, that every star may perchance be another world, yet I would not swear that it is so; but I will believe it to be true, because that opinion is so pleasant to me, and gives me very diverting ideas, which have fixed themselves delightfully in my imaginations, and 'tis necessary that even solid truth should have its agreeableness.'

'Well,' said she, 'since your folly is so pleasing to you, give me a share of it; I will believe whatever you please concerning the stars, if I find it pleasant.'

'Ah, Madam,' said I, hastily, 'it is not such a pleasure as you find one of Molière's plays; it is a pleasure that is – I know not where in our reason and which only transports the mind.'

'What?' replied she, 'do you think me then incapable of all those pleasures which entertain our reason, and only treat the mind? I will instantly show you the contrary, at least as soon as you have told me what you know of your stars.'

'Ah, Madam,' cried I, 'I shall never endure to be reproached with that neglect of my own happiness, that in a grove at ten o'clock of the night, I talked of nothing but philosophy, to the greatest beauty in the world; no Madam, search for philosophy somewhere else.'

But 'twas in vain to put her off by excuses, from a novelty she was already but too much prepossessed with: there was a necessity of yielding, and all I could do was to prevail with her to be secret, for the saving my honour; but when I found myself engaged past retreat, and had a design to speak, I knew not where to begin my discourse for to prove to her (who understood nothing of natural philosophy) that the Earth was a planet, and all the other planets so many Earths, and all the stars worlds, it was necessary for the explaining myself, to bring my arguments a great way off; and therefore I still endeavoured to persuade her that 'twas much better to pass the time in another manner of conversation, which the most reasonable people in our circumstances would do; but I pleaded to no purpose, and at last to satisfy her, and give her a general idea of philosophy, I made use of this way of arguing.

'All philosophy is grounded on two principles, that of a passionate thirst of knowledge of the mind, and the weakness of the organs of the body; for if the eyesight were in perfection, you could as easily discern there were worlds in the stars, as that there are stars. On the other hand, if you were less curious and desirous of knowledge, you would be indifferent whether it were so or not, which indeed comes all to the same purpose; but we would gladly know more than we see, and there's the difficulty: for if we could see well and truly what we see, we should know enough; but we see most objects quite otherwise than they are; so that the true philosophers spend their time in not believing what they see, and in endeavouring to guess at the knowledge of what they see not; and in my opinion this kind of life is not much to be envied; but I fancy still to myself that nature is a great scene, or representation, much like one of our operas; for, from the place where you sit to behold the opera, you do not see the stage, as really it is, since everything is disposed there for the representing agreeable objects to your sight, from a large distance, while the wheels and weights which move and counterpoise the machines are all concealed from our view; nor do we trouble ourselves so much to find out how all those motions that we see there are performed; and it may be among so vast a number of spectators, there is not above one engineer in the whole pit, that troubles himself with the consideration how those flights are managed that seem so new and so extra-ordinary to him, and who resolves at any rate to find out the contrivance of them. You cannot but guess, Madam, that this engineer is not unlike a philosopher; but that which makes the difficulty incomparably greater to philosophers, is, that the ropes, pulleys, wheels and weights which give motion to the different scenes represented to us by nature, are so well hid both from our sight and understanding, that it was a long time before mankind could so much as guess at the causes that moved the vast frame of the universe.

'Pray, Madam, imagine to yourself, the ancient philosophers beholding one of our operas such and a one as Pythagoras, Plato, Aristotle, and many more whose names and reputations make so great a noise in the world; and suppose they were to behold the flying of Phaeton, who is carried aloft by the winds, and that they could not discern the ropes and pulleys, but were altogether ignorant of the contrivance of the machine behind the scenes; one of them would be apt to say, "it is a certain secret virtue that carries up Phaeton."

'Another: "That Phaeton is composed of certain numbers, which make him mount upwards."

'The third: "That Phaeton has a certain kindness for the biggest part of the theatre, and is uneasy when he is not there."

'And a fourth: "That Phaeton was not made for flying, but that he had rather fly, than leave the upper part of the stage void."

'Besides a hundred other notions, which I wonder have not entirely ruined the reputation of the ancients. In our age, Descartes, and some other moderns would say, "That Phaeton's flight upward is because he is hoisted by ropes and that while he ascends, a greater weight than he descends."

'And now men do not believe that any corporeal being moves itself, unless it be set in motion or pushed by another body, or drawn by ropes; nor that any heavy thing ascends or descends, without a counterpoise equal with it in weight to balance it; or that 'tis guided by springs. And could we see nature as it is, we should see nothing but the hinder part of the theatre at the opera.'

'By what you say,' said Madam la Marquise, 'philosophy is become very mechanical.'

'So very mechanical,' said I, 'that I am afraid men will quickly be ashamed of it; for some would have the universe no other thing in great, than a watch is in little; and that all in it are ordered by regular motion, which depends upon the just and equal disposal of its parts. Confess the truth, Madam, have not you honoured it with a better opinion than it deserved?'

'I have known several esteem it less since they believed they knew it better; and for my part,' said she, 'I esteem it more since I knew it is so like a watch. And 'tis most surprising to me, that the course and order of nature, however admirable it appears to be, moves upon principles and things that are so very easy and simple.'

'I know not,' replied I, 'who has given you so just ideas of it, but 'tis not ordinary to have such; most people retain in their minds some false principle or other of admiration, wrapped up in obscurity, which they adore. They admire nature only because they look on it as a kind of miracle, which they do not understand; and 'tis certain that those sort of people never despise anything, but from the moment they begin to understand it. But, Madam, I find you so well disposed to comprehend all I have to say to you, that without further preface, I need only draw the curtain, and show you the world.

'From the Earth where we are, that which we see at the greatest distance from us, is that azure heaven, or vast vault, where the stars are placed as so many golden nails, which are called fixed, because they seem to have no other motion, but that of their proper sphere, which carries them along with it, from east to west; between the Earth and the last, or lowest heaven, are hung at different heights, the Sun, the Moon, and five other stars, which are called planets, Mercury, Venus, Mars, Jupiter and Saturn. These planets not being fixed to any one sphere, and having unequal motions, they are in different aspects, one to another, and according as they are in conjunction, or at distance, they make different figures; whereas the fixed stars are always in the same position, one towards another. As for example, Charles' Wain or the constellation of the Great Bear, which you see, and which consists of seven stars, has always been, and will still continue the same; but the Moon is sometimes near the Sun, and sometimes at a great distance from it, and so through all the rest of the planets.

It was in this manner that the celestial bodies appeared to the ancient Chaldean shepherds, whose great leisure produced these first observations, which have since been so well improved; and upon which all astronomy is founded. For astronomy has its beginnings in Chaldea, as geometry was invented in Egypt, where the inundations of the River Nile, having confounded and removed the limits and the landmarks of the several possessions of the inhabitants, did prompt them to find out sure and exact measures, by which everyone might know his own field from that of his neighbours. So that astronomy is the daughter of idleness, geometry is the child of interest; and should we inquire into the original of poetry, we should in all appearance find that it owes its beginnings to love.'

'I am extremely glad,' said the Marquise, 'that I have learned the genealogy of the sciences, and I find that I must content myself with astronomy, geometry, according to what you have said, requiring a soul more interested in worldly concerns, than I am, and for poetry, 'tis most proper for those of a more amorous inclination, but I have all the leisure and time to spare that astronomy requires: besides that I live now happily retired in the fields and groves, and lead a sort of pastoral life, so very agreeable to astronomy.'

'Do not deceive yourself, Madam,' said I; ''tis not a true pastoral life, to talk of planets and fixed stars: be pleased to consider, that the shepherds in the story of Astraea did not pass their time in that kind of divertissement; they had business of a softer and more agreeable nature.'

'Oh,' said she, 'the life of the pastorals of Astraea is too dangerous. I like that of the Chaldean shepherds better, of whom you spoke but now: go on with them, for I will hear nothing from you, but Chaldean. So soon as that order and these motions of the heavens were discovered, what was the next thing to be considered?'

'The next thing,' said I, 'was to guess how the several parts of the universe were to be disposed and ranged in order, and that is what the learned call, "the making of a system". But before, Madam, I explain to you the first system, be pleased to observe that we are all naturally made like a certain Athenian fool, of whom you have heard, who fancied that all the ships that came into the port of Piraeus, belonged to him; for we are so vain as to believe, that all this vast frame of nature was defined to our use. For if a philosopher be asked, for what all this prodigious number of fixed stars serve (since a very few would supply the business of the whole) he will tell you gravely, that they were made to please our sight. Upon this principle, as first, man believed that the Earth was immoveably fixed in the centre of the universe, whilst all the celestial bodies (made only for her) were at the pains of turning continually round, to give light to the Earth: and that it was therefore above the Earth, they placed the Moon; above the Moon, Mercury; then Venus, the Sun, Mars, Jupiter, Saturn; and above all, the sphere of the fixed stars. The Earth, according to this opinion, was just in the middle of several circles, described by the planets; and the greater these circles were, the further they were distant from the Earth; and by consequence, they took a longer time in completing their round; which is certainly true.'

'I know not,' said the Marquise, 'why you should not approve of this order of the universe, which seems to be so clear and intelligible; for my part, I am extremely pleased and satisfied with it.'

'Madam,' said I, 'without vanity, I have very much softened and explained this system: should I expose it to you such as it was first invented by its author Ptolemy, or by those that have followed his principles, it would frighten you. The motion of the planets being irregular, they move sometimes fast, sometimes slow; sometimes towards one side, sometimes to another; at one time near the Earth, at another far from it. The ancients did imagine I know not how many circles, differently interwoven one with another; by which they fancied to themselves, they understood all the irregular phenomena, or appearances in nature. And the conclusion of these circles was so great that, at that time, when men knew no better, a king of Aragon, a great mathematician (not over-devout) said that if God had called him to his council when he formed the universe, he could have given him good advice. The thought was impious, yet 'tis odd to reflect, that the confusion of Ptolemy's system gave an occasion for the sin of that king: the good advice he would have given was, no doubt, for surpassing these different circles, which had so embarrassed the celestial motions; and, it may be also, with regard to the two or three superfluous spheres, which they had placed above the fixed stars. The philosophers, to explain the kind of motion of the heavenly bodies, did fancy a sphere of crystal above that heaven which we see, which set the inferior heaven in motion; and if anyone made a new discovery of any other motion, they immediately made a new sphere of crystal: in short, these crystalline heavens cost them nothing.

'But why spheres of crystal?' said Madam la Marquise. 'Would no other substance serve?'

'No,' said I, 'Madam; for there was a necessity of their being transparent, that the light might penetrate; as it was requisite for them to be solid bodies. Aristotle had found out that solidity was inherent in the excellence of their nature; and because he said it, nobody would adventure to question the truth of it. But there have appeared comets, which we know to have been vastly higher from the Earth, than was believed by the ancients. These in their course would have broke all those crystal spheres; and indeed must have ruined the universe: so that there was an absolute necessity to believe the heavens to be made of a fluid substance; at last, 'tis not to be doubted, from the observation of this, and the last age, that Venus and Mercury move round the Sun, and not round the Earth. So that the ancient system is not to be defended, as to this particular. But I will propose one to you, which solves all objections, and which will put the King of Aragon out of condition of advising; and which is so surprisingly simple and easy, that that good quality alone ought to make it preferable to all others.'

'Methinks,' said Madam la Marquise, 'that your philosophy is a kind of sale, or farm, where those that offer to do the affair at the smallest expense are preferred.'

''Tis very true,' said I; 'and 'tis only by that, that we are able to guess at the scheme upon which nature hath framed her work: she is very saving, and will take the shortest and cheapest way. Yet notwithstanding, this frugality is accompanied with a most surprising magnificence, which shines in all she has done; but the magnificence is in the design, and the economy of the execution: and indeed there is nothing finer than a great design, carried on with a little expense. But we are very apt to overturn all these operations of nature, by contrary ideas. We put economy in the design, and magnificence in the execution: we give her a little design, which we make her perform with ten times a greater charge than is needful.'

'I shall be very glad,' said she, 'that this system you are to speak of will imitate nature so exactly; for this good husbandry will turn to the advantage of my understanding, since by it

I shall have less trouble to comprehend what you have to say. There is in this system no more unnecessary difficulties.'

'Know then, that a certain German, named Copernicus, does at one blow cut off all these different circles, and crystalline spheres, invented by the ancients; destroying the one; and breaks the other in pieces; and being inspired with a noble astronomical fury, takes the Earth, and hangs it at a vast distance from the centre of the world, and sets the Sun in its place, to whom that honour does more properly belong: the planets do no longer turn around the Earth, nor do they any longer contain it in the circle they describe; and if they enlighten us, it is by chance, and because they find us in their way. All things now turn round the Sun; among which, the globe itself, to punish it for the long rest, so falsely attributed to it before; and Copernicus has loaded the Earth with all those motions formerly attributed to the other planets; having left this little globe none of the celestial train, save only the Moon, whose natural course it is, to turn round the Earth.'

'Soft and fair,' said Madam la Marquise; 'you are in so great a rapture, and express yourself with so much pomp and eloquence, I hardly understand what you mean. You place the Sun unmoveable in the centre of the universe; pray what follows next?'

'Mercury,' said I, 'who turns around the Sun: next comes the Earth; which being more elevated than Mercury or Venus describes a circle of greater circumference than those two planets. Last, come Mars, Jupiter, Saturn, in their order, as I have named them. So that you see easily, that Saturn ought to make the greatest circle round the Sun; it is therefore that Saturn takes more time to make his revolution, than any other planet.'

'Ah,' said the Marquise, interrupting me, 'you forget the Moon.'

'Do not fear,' said I, 'Madam; I shall soon find her again. The Moon turns round the Earth, and never leaves it; and as the Earth moves in the circle it describes round the Sun, the Moon follows the Earth, in turning round it; and if the Moon do move round the Sun, it is only because she will not abandon the Earth.'

'I understand you,' said she. 'I love the Moon for staying with us, when all the other planets have left us; and you must confess, that your German Copernicus would have taken her from us too, had it been in his power; for I perceive by his procedure, he had no great kindness for the Earth.'

'I am extremely pleased with him,' said I, 'for having humbled the vanity of mankind, who had usurped the first and best situation in the universe; and I am glad to see the Earth under the same circumstances with the other planets.'

'That's very fine,' said the Marquise. 'Do you believe that the vanity of man places itself in astronomy; or that I am any way humbled, because you tell me the Earth turns around the Sun? I'll swear I do not esteem myself one whit the less.'

'Good Lord, Madam,' said I, 'do you think I can imagine you can be as zealous for a precedency in the universe, as you would be for that in a chamber? No, Madam; the rank of place between two planets will never make such a bustle in the world, as that of two ambassadors. Nevertheless, the same inclination that makes us endeavour to have the first place in a ceremony, prevails with a philosopher in composing his system, to place himself in the centre of the world, if he can. He is proud to fancy all things made for himself; and without reflection, flatters his sense with this opinion, which consists purely of speculation.'

'Oh,' said the Marquise, 'this is a calumny of your own invention against mankind, which ought never to have received Copernicus his opinion, since so easy and so humble.'

'Copernicus,' said I, 'Madam, himself was the most diffident of his own system; so that it was a long time before he would venture to publish it, and at last resolved to do it at the earnest entreaty of people of the first quality. But do you know what he did, the day they brought him the first printed copy of his book? That he might not be troubled to answer all the objections and contradictions he was sure to meet with, he wisely left the world and died.'

'Hold,' said the Marquise, 'we ought to do justice to all the world; and 'tis more certain, 'tis very hard to believe we turn round, since we do not change places, and that we find ourselves in the morning, where we lay down the night before. I see very well by your looks, what 'tis you are going to say; that since the Earth moves all together –'

'Most certainly,' said I: ''Tis the same thing as if you were asleep in a boat, sailing on a river, you would find yourself in the same place in the morning, and in the same situation as to the several parts of the boat.'

'True,' said she, 'but with this difference; I should, at my waking, find another shore; and that would convince me, my boat had changed its situation. But 'tis not the same with the Earth; for there I find everything as I left it the night before.'

'Not at all, Madam,' said I; 'the Earth changes the shore, as well as your boat. You know, Madam, that above and beyond the circles, described by the planets, is the sphere of the fixed stars; that's our shore. I am on the Earth, which makes a great circle around the Sun; I look toward the centre of this circle, there I see the Sun; if the brightness of his rays did not remove the stars from my sight, by looking in a straight line, I should easily perceive the Sun corresponding to some fixed star beyond him; but in the night-time, I see clearly the stars, to which the Sun did answer, or was opposite to, the day before; which is, indeed, the same thing. If the Earth were immoveable, and did not alter its situation in its own circle, I should always see the Sun opposite the same fixed stars; but I see the Sun in different opposition to the stars, every day of the year. It most necessarily follows then, the Earth changes its situation, that is, the shore, round which we go daily. And a the Earth performs its revolution in a year, I see the Sun, in that space of time, answer in direct opposition to a whole circle of fixed stars; this circle is called the zodiac: will you please, Madam, that I trace the figure of it on the sand?'

'By no means,' said she, 'I can satisfy myself, without the demonstration: besides that, it would give a certain mathematical air to my park, which I do not like. Have not I heard of a certain philosopher, who being shipwrecked and cast upon an unknown island; who seeing some mathematical proportions drawn on the sea sands, called to one of those with him, and cries, "Courage my friends, here are footsteps of men; this country is inhabited"? You know, it is not decent in me to make such footsteps, nor must they be seen in this place.'

''Tis fit,' continued I, 'Madam, that nothing be seen here, but the steps of lovers; that is to say, your name and cipher engraven on the bark of trees by the hand of your adorers.'

'Pray, Sir,' said she, 'let adorers alone, and let us speak of the Sun. I understand very well, how we imagine he describes that circle, which indeed we ourselves describe; but this requires a whole year's time, when one would think the Sun passes over our heads every day. How comes that to pass?'

'Have you not observed,' said I, 'that a bowl thrown on the Earth, has two different motions; it runs toward the jack, to which it is thrown; and at the same time it turns over and over several times, before it comes that length; so that you will see the mark that is on the bowl, sometimes above, and sometimes below. 'Tis just so with the Earth; in the time it advances on the circle it makes round the Sun, in its yearly course, it turns over once every four and twenty hours, upon its own axis; so that in that space of time, which is one natural day, every point of the Earth (which is not near the South or North Poles) loses and recovers the sight of the sun. And as we turn towards the Sun, we imagine that the Sun is rising upon us; so when we turn from it, we believe she is setting.'

'This is very pleasant,' said the Marquise. 'You make the circle to do all, and the Sun to stand idle; and when we see the Moon, planets and fixed stars turn round us in four and twenty hours, all is but bare imagination.'

'Nothing else,' said I, 'but pure fancy, which proceeds from the same cause; only the planets make their circle round the Sun, not in the same space of time, but according to their unequal distance from it; and that planet which we see today, look to a certain point of the zodiac, or sphere of fixed stars, we shall see it answer to an other point tomorrow; as well because that planet moves on its course, as that we proceed in ours. We move, and so do the other planets: by this means we vary both situation and opposition, as to them, and we think we discover irregularities in their revolutions, which I will not trouble you with; 'tis sufficient for you to know, that anything that may appear to us to be irregular, in the course of the planets, is occasioned by our own motion meeting theirs in such different manners; but upon the whole the course of the planets, is most regular.'

'I agree with all my heart,' said the Marquise; 'yet I wish with all my heart, that that regularity were not so laborious to the Earth: I fancy Copernicus has not been very careful of its concerns, in making so weighty and solid a mass run about so nimbly.'

'But, Madam,' said I, 'would you rather that the Sun, and the stars (which are generally far greater bodies) should make a vast circumference round the Earth in a day, and run an infinite number of leagues in twenty-four hours time? Which they must of necessity do, if the Earth have not that diurnal motion on its own axis.'

'Oh!' answered she, 'the Sun and the stars are all fire, swiftness of motion is easy to them; but of the Earth, that does seem to be very portable.'

'And would you believe it,' said I, 'Madam, if you had never seen the experiment, that a first-rate ship, of a hundred and twenty guns, with fifteen hundred men, and proportional provision, with all her ammunition and tackle aboard, were a very portable thing? Notwithstanding, a gentle breeze will move this ship on the sea, because the water is liquid, and yielding easily, makes no resistance to the motion of the vessel. So the Earth, notwithstanding of its vast bulk and weight, is easily moved in the celestial matter, which is a thousand times more fluid than the water of the sea; and which fills all that vast extent, where the planets swim, as it were. And to what would you fix or grapple the Earth to hinder it from being carried along with the current of this celestial matter or substance? It would be just as if a little wooden ball should not follow the current of a rapid river.'

'But,' said she, 'how does the Earth support its vast weight, on your heavenly substance, which ought to be very light, since it is to be fluid?'

'That does not follow,' answered I, 'Madam, that a thing must be light, because it is fluid: what say you to the first-rate ship, I spoke of with all its lading. Yet 'tis lighter than the water, because it swims upon it.'

'As long as you command your first-rate frigate,' said she, angrily, 'I will not argue with you; but can you assure me, that I am in no danger by inhabiting such a little humming-top, as you have made the world to be?'

'Well, Madam,' said I, 'the Earth shall be supported by four elephants, as the Indians fancy it is.'

'Here's a new system indeed,' cried Madam la Marquise; 'yet I love those men, for providing for their own security, by resting upon a solid foundation; whereas we that follow Copernicus are so inconsiderate as to swim at a venture upon your celestial matter. And I dare say, if these Indians thought the Earth in any danger of falling, they would quickly double the number of their elephants.'

'They would have all the reason in the world to do so,' said I (laughing at her fancy), 'Madam; and would not spare elephants to sleep in quiet, without fear of falling: and, Madam, we will add as many as you please to our system this night, and take them away by degrees, as you get more assurance.'

'Really,' said she, 'I do not think that they are needful at present; upon this system you will form to yourself very pleasant and agreeable ideas: as for example sometimes I fancy I am hanging in the air, and that I stay there without moving, while the Earth turns round under me in four and twenty hours time, and that I see beneath me all those different faces; some white, some black, some tawny, others of an olive colour; first I see hats, then turbans, there heads covered with wool, there shaved heads; sometimes towns with steeple, some with their long small-pointed pyramids, and half-moons on their tops; sometimes towns with porcelain towers; after them, spacious fields, without towns, only tents and huts; here vast seas, frightful deserts; in short, all the variety that is to be seen upon the face of the Earth.

'Indeed,' said she, 'such a sight would be very well worth twenty-four hours of one's time. So that by this system, through the same place where we now are (I do not mean this park, but that space of air which our bodies fill) several other nations must successively pass, and we return hither in twenty-four hours, to our own place again.'

'Copernicus himself,' said I, 'Madam, did not understand it better. At first will be here the English, discoursing, it may be, upon some politic design, with more gravity, but less pleasure than we talk of our philosophy. Next will come a vast ocean, in which there will be sailing some ships, perhaps not so much at their ease as we are. Then will appear the cannibals, eating some prisoners of war alive, they seeming very unconcerned at what they suffer: after them, the women of the country of Jesso, who spend all their time in preparing their husbands meals, and in painting their lips and eyebrows with blue, to please the ugliest fellows in the world. Next will succeed the Tartars who go, with great devotion, on pilgrimage to that great priest, who never comes out of an obscure place, where he has no other light but lamps, by which they adore him. After them, the beautiful Circassian women who make no difficulty of granting any favour to the first comer, except what they essential know does belong to their husbands. Then the Crim, or little Tartars, who live by stealing of wives for the Turks and Persians. And at last, ourselves again, perhaps talking as we do now.'

'I am mightily taken,' said the Marquise, 'with the fancy of what you say; but if I could see all these things from above,

I would wish to have the power to hasten and stop the motion of the Earth, according as I liked or disliked the several objects that pass under me; I would make the politicians, and those that eat their enemies, to move very fast. But there are others that I should be very curious to observe; and particularly, the fine Circassian women who have one so peculiar a custom.'

'That is,' said I, 'their husbands, who, finding so many charms in their embraces, as more than satisfy them, do freely abandon their fair wives to strangers.'

'The women of our country,' said the Marquise, 'must be very ugly if compared to the Circassians; for our husbands will part for nothing.'

'That is the reason,' said I, 'that the more is taken from 'em; whereas –'

'No more of these fooleries,' said the Marquise, interrupting me; 'there's a serious difficulty come into my head: if the Earth turn around, then we change air every moment, and must breath still that of another country.'

'By no means, Madam,' said I; 'the air which encompasses the Earth extends itself to a certain height, it may be about two or three leagues, and turns round with us. You have, no doubt, seen a thousand times the business of the silkworm, where the balls which these little creatures do work with so much art, for their own imprisonment, are compact, and wrought together with silk, which is very closely joined; but they are covered with a kind of down, that is very light and soft. Thus it is that the Earth, which is solid, is wrapped in a covering of soft down of two or thre leagues thickness, which is the air that is carried round at the same time with it. Above the air is that celestial matter I spoke of, incomparably more pure, more subtle, and more agitated than the air.'

'You represent the Earth to me,' said the Marquise, 'as a very contemptible thing, by the despicable ideas you give me of it: 'tis, nevertheless, upon this silkworm-ball, there are performed such mighty works; and where there are such terrible wars, and such strange commotions as reign everywhere.'

''Tis certainly true,' said I, 'Madam; while at the same time, nature, who is not at the pains to consider these troubles and commotions, carries us along together, by a general motion, and does as it were play with this little glove.'

'It seems to me,' said she, 'that 'tis very ridiculous to inhabit fanything that turns so often, and is so much agitated; and the worst of all is, that we are not assured whether we turn round, or not; for, to be plain with you, and that I may keep none of my doubts from you, I do extremely suspect, that all the precautions you can take, will not convince me of the motion of the Earth: for is it possible, but nature would have taken care to have given us some sensible sign, by which we might discover the turning round of so vast a body?'

'The motions,' answered I, 'which are most natural are the least perceptible; and which holds true, even in morality; for the motion of self-love is so natural to us, that for the most part we do not feel it, while we believe we act by other principles.'

'Ah,' said she, 'do you begin to speak of moral philosophy, when the question is of that which is altogether natural? But I perceive you are sleepy, and begin to yawn; let us therefore retire, for there's enough said for the first night, tomorrow we shall return hither again; you with your systems, and I with my ignorance.'

In returning to the castle to make an end of what might be said to systems, I told her, there was a third opinion invented by Tycho Brahe, who would have the Earth absolutely immoveable, and made the Sun to turn round it, as he did the other planets to turn around the sun; because, since the new discoveries, it could not be imagined that the other planets turned around the Earth. But my lady Marquise, whose judgement and understanding is solid and penetrating, found there was too much affectation in endeavouring to free the Earth from turning round the Sun, since several other great bodies could not be exempt from the labour; and that the Sun was not so proper and fit to turn round the Earth, since the other planets turn round the Sun; and that this new system was only good to maintain the standing still of the Earth, if one had a mind to undertake that argument; but 'tis not proper to persuade another to believe it. At last, we resolved to hold ourselves to the opinion of Copernicus which is more uniform and more agreeable, without the least mixture of prejudice; and, indeed, its simplicity and easiness persuades as much as its boldness pleads.

THE SECOND NIGHT

As soon as one could get into my lady Marquise's apartments, I sent to know how she did, and how she had slept that night in turning round. She sent me word, that now she was pretty accustomed to the motion of the Earth, and that Copernicus himself could not have rested better that night than she did. A little after this, there came company to visit my lady, which, according to the nauseous country fashion, stayed till the evening, and yet we thought ourselves happy that we were so easily rid of 'em then, since, according to the custom of the country, they might have prolonged their visit till the next day; but they were so civil, as not to do it; so that Madam the Marquise and I found ourselves at liberty. In the evening we went again to the park, and the conversation began as it ended before, of our system: my lady Marquise had comprehended 'em so well, that she would not be at pains to reassume anything of what had passed, but pressed me to lead her to something that was new.

'Well,' said I, 'since the Sun, which is now immoveable, and no longer a planet; and that the Earth, that moves round the Sun, is now one, be not surprised if I tell you, the Moon is another Earth, and is, by all appearance, inhabited.'

Said she, 'I never heard of the Moon's being inhabited, but as a fable.'

'So it may be still,' said I. 'I concern myself no further in these matters, than men used to do in the civil wars; where the uncertainty of what may be, makes people still entertain a correspondence with the adverse party. As for me, though I see the Moon inhabited, I live very civilly with those that do not believe it; and I carry myself so trimmingly, that I may, upon occasion, with honour go over to their side who have the better; but still they gain some considerable advantage over us. I'll tell you my reasons that make me take part with the inhabitants of the Moon: suppose then, there had never been any commerce between Paris and Saint-Denis, and that a citizen of Paris, who had never been out of that city, should go up to the top of the steeple of Our Lady, and should view Saint-Denis at a distance, and one should ask him if he believed Saint-Denis to be inhabited; he would answer boldly, "Not at all; for," he would say, "I see the inhabitants of Paris, but I do not see those of Saint-Denis, nor ever heard of 'em." It may be, somebody standing by would represent to him, that it was true, one could not see the inhabitants of Saint-Denis from Our Lady's Church, but that the distance was the cause of it; yet that all we could see of Saint-Denis, was very like to Paris; for Saint-Denis had steeples, houses and walls; and that it might resemble Paris in everything else, and be inhabited as well as it. All these arguments would not prevail upon my citizen; who would continue still obstinate in maintaining that Saint-Denis was not inhabited, because he saw none of the people. The Moon is our Saint-Denis, and we are the citizens of Paris, that never went out of our own town.'

'Ah,' interrupted the Marquise, 'you do us wrong; we are not so foolish as your citizens of Paris: since he sees that Saint-Denis is so like to Paris in everything, he must have lost his reason, if he did not think it was inhabited. But for the Moon, that is nothing like the Earth.'

'Have a care, Madam,' said I, 'what you say; for if I make it appear, that the Moon is in every thing like the Earth, you are obliged to believe that the Moon is inhabited.'

'I acknowledge,' said she, 'if you do that, I must yield; and your looks are so assured that you frighten me already. The two different motions of the Earth, which would never have entered my thoughts, make me very apprehensive of all you say. But is it possible that the Earth can be an enlightened body, as the Moon is? For, to resemble it, it must be so.'

'Alas, Madam,' said I, 'to be enlightened, is not so great a matter as you imagine, and the Sun only is remarkable for that quality: 'tis he alone that is enlightened of himself, by virtue of his particular essence; but the other planets shine only as being enlightened by the Sun: the Sun communicates his light to the Moon, which reflects it upon the Earth; as the Earth, without doubt, reflects it back again to the Moon, since the distance from the Moon to the Earth is the same as from the Earth to the Moon.'

'But,' said the Marquise, 'is the Earth as proper for reflecting the light of the Sun, as the Moon?'

'You are always for the Moon,' said I, 'and you cannot rid yourself of those remains of kindness you have for her. Light is composed of little balls, which rebound upon any solid body, which is opaque, or obscure, and are sent back another way; whereas they pass through anything that offers an opening, or passage, in a straight line; which is diaphanous, or clear; such as air and glass: so that the Moon enlightens us, because it is an opaque, solid body, which retorts these little balls upon us; and I believe you will not dispute the same solidity to the Earth. Admire then, Madam, how advantageous it is, to be well posted; so that the Moon being at a great distance from us, we see it as an enlightened body only, but are ignorant that 'tis a gross, solid mass, very much like the Earth. On the other hand, the Earth having the ill luck to be seen by us too near, we consider it only a great massy body, fit only for the producing of food for living creatures.'

''Tis just,' said the Marquise, 'as when we are struck and surprised with the splendour of quality above our own; we do not perceive, that in the main, there is no difference between them and us.'

''Tis just so,' said I; 'and we will needs be judging of everything; but we have the misfortune, still to be placed in a false light. Would we judge of ourselves, we are too near: if of others, we are too far off: could one be placed between the Moon and the Earth that would be true station to consider both well. To this end, we ought only to be spectators of the world, and not inhabitants.'

'I shall never be satisfied,' said the Marquise, 'with the injury we do the Earth, in being too favourably engaged for the inhabitants of the Moon, unless you can assure me that they are as ignorant of their advantages, as we are of ours; and that they take our Earth for a star, without knowing that the globe they inhabit is one also.'

'Be assured of that, Madam,' said I, 'that the Earth appears to them to perform all the functions of a star. 'Tis true, they do not see the Earth describe a circle round 'em, but that's all one; I'll explain to you what it is: that side of the Moon which was turned towards the Earth at the beginning of the world, has continued towards the Earth ever since; which still represents to us these same eyes, nose and mouth, which our imagination fancies we see composed of these spots, lights and shadows, which are the surface of the Moon: could we see the other half of the Moon, 'tis possible our fancy would represent to us some other figure. This does not argue, but the Moon turns however upon her own axis, and takes as much time to perform that revolution, as she does to go round the Earth in a month. But then, when the Moon performs a part of her revolutions on her own axis, and that she ought to hide from us (for example) one cheek of this imaginary face, and appear to us in another position, she does at the same time perform as much of the circle she describes in turning round the Earth; and though she is in a new point of sight or opposition as to us, yet she represents to us still the same cheek: so that the Moon, in regard to the Sun, and the other planets, turns upon her own axis; but does not so as to the Earth.

'The inhabitants of the Moon see all the other planets rise and set in the space of fifteen days, but they see our Earth always hanging in the same point of the heavens. This seeming immoveability does not very well agree with a body that ought to pass for a planet; but the truth is the Earth is not in such perfection. Besides the Moon has a certain trembling quality, which does sometimes hide a little of her imaginary face, and at other times shows a little of her opposite side; and no doubt but the inhabitants of the Moon attribute this shaking to the Earth, and believe we make a certain swinging in the heavens, like the pendulum of a clock.'

'All these planets,' said the Marquise, 'are like to us mortals, who always cast our own faults upon others. Says the Earth, "It is not I that turn round, 'tis the Sun." Says the Moon, "It is not I that tremble, 'tis the Earth." There are errors and mistakes everywhere.'

'I would not advise you,' said I, 'to undertake to reform any of 'em; 'tis better that I make an end in convincing you, that the Moon is in all things like the Earth. Represent to yourself these two great globes, hanging in the heavens; you know that the Sun does always enlighten one half of any globe, and the other half is in the shadow; there is therefore always one half of both Moon and Earth that is enlightened, or hat day. And the other half is still in the darkness of night. Be pleased, besides, to consider that a ball has less force and swiftness after it rebounds from a wall, against which it was thrown, than it had before it touched the wall, which sends it another way; so light is not so strong, after 'tis reflected by any solid body: this pale light which comes to us from the Moon, is the light of the Sun itself, but we have it only by reflection from the Moon, and has lost a great deal of that strength and vivacity which it had when 'twas received by the Moon, directly from the Sun; and that bright and dazzling light which we receive from the Sun, must in the same manner appear to the inhabitants of the Moon, after 'tis reflected by the Earth, on the Moon. So that the surface of the Moon, which we see enlightened, and which shines upon us in the night, is that half of the Moon that enjoys the day, as that half of the globe of the Earth which is enlightened by the Sun, when 'tis turned towards the darkness half of the globe of the Moon, does give light to the inhabitants there, during their nights. All depends upon the different opposition and aspects between the Moon and the Earth. The first and second day of the Moon, we do not see her, because she is betwixt the Sun and us, and moves with the Sun by our day; it necessarily follows, that the half of the Moon which is enlightened, is turned towards the Sun, and the obscure part towards the Earth; 'tis no wonder then, that we cannot see that half which is dark; by that same half of the Moon which is in darkness, being turned towards the enlightened half of the Earth, the inhabitants see us, without being seen, and the Earth appears to them, as their full Moon does to us; and so, if one may use the expression, 'tis with them full Earth. After this, the Moon going on in her monthly circle, disengages herself from the Sun, and begins to turn towards us a part of her enlightened half, which is the crescent; at the very same time, the darkened half of the Moon loses some share of the enlightened part of the Earth, and then the Earth is in the wane, as to its inhabitants.'

'Say no more,' said the Marquise, briskly, 'I shall know all the rest when I please; I need only think a little, and follow the

Moon in her monthly circle. I see, in general, that the inhabitants of the Moon have their month, the exact reverse of ours, and I am persuaded, when 'tis full Moon, the enlightened half of it is turned towards the obscure part of the Earth, and then they do not see us, but say it is a new Earth. I would not have anybody reproach me with the want of so much sense, as that you need to explain so easy a thing to me. But as to the eclipses, what is the cause of them?'

'If you do not understand that,' said I, ''tis your own fault. When 'tis the new Moon, and she is between the Sun and the Earth, and that all her obscure half is turned towards us, who then enjoy the day, you may see easily that the shadow of this darkened half is cast upon the Earth; if the Moon be directly under the Sun, this shadow hides the Sun from us, and at the same time, darkens a part of the enlightened half of the Earth, which was seen by the inhabitants of the obscure side of the Moon: and this is an eclipse of the Sun to us, in our day; and an eclipse of the Earth to those in the Moon, in their night. When the Moon is at the full, the Earth is betwixt her and the Sun, and all the obscure part of the Earth is turned towards the enlightened half of the Moon, the shadow of the Earth is then cast upon the Moon; and if it falls directly on her surface, it obscures the enlightened half which we see, and hides the Sun from that enlightened part of the Moon that enjoyed the day: this is an eclipse of the Moon to us, during our night; and an eclipse of the Sun to them, during their day. By this reason, it falls out that there are not always eclipses when the Moon interposes between the Sun and the Earth, or the Earth is interjected between the Sun and the Moon; because these three bodies are not opposite one to another, in a straight line; and by consequence, that of the three, which ought to make the eclipse, casts its shadow a little to one side of that which should be eclipsed.'

'I am extremely surprised,' said the Marquise, 'that (since there is so little of mystery or difficulty in eclipses) everybody does not find out the cause of 'em.'

'Do not wonder at that,' said I, 'Madam; there are many nations in the world, that, as they go to work, will not find out for ages to come; for all over the East Indias, the inhabitants believe that when the Sun or Moon is eclipsed, certain demons, or spirits, who have very black claws, do stretch them forth upon these two luminaries, which he endeavours to seize: and during the time of the eclipse, you may see all the rivers covered with heads of Indians; for they go into the water, up to the neck, thinking that most devout posture for obtaining from the Sun and Moon a defence against that demon. In America, the people were persuaded that the Sun and the Moon were angry with 'em when they were eclipsed; and God knows what pains they are at to make their peace with 'em. But the Greeks, who were so polite a people, did not they believe for a long time, that the Moon was bewitched, and that the magicians made her come down to throw a certain poisonous scum or dew upon the herbs and grass? And even we ourselves, were we not frightened out of our wits at an eclipse of the Sun that happened about thirty years since? Did not a great many people shut themselves up in vaults and cellars? And did not the learned men write in vain to assure us there was no danger?'

'Certainly,' said the Marquise, 'that's very disgraceful to mankind; and I think there ought to be a law made by universal consent, never to speak of eclipses hereafter, lest the memory of such folly should be preserved to posterity.'

'Pray, Madam,' said I, 'let there be another law made for abolishing the memory of all things past; for I know of nothing that is not a monument of the folly of mankind.'

'Pray, tell me,' said the Marquise; 'are the inhabitants of the Moon as much afraid of eclipses as we are? It seems to me very ridiculous, that some of 'em should run into the water up the neck; that others should think our Earth should be bewitched, and that we coming to spoil their grass.'

'Without all doubt,' said I, 'Madam: why should the inhabitants of the Moon have more sense than we? And what right have they to frighten us, more than we have to frighten them? Nay, more; I am apt to believe that as there has been, and still are, many inhabitants in our globe who are such fools to adore the Moon; there are also inhabitants in the Moon, foolish enough to adore our Earth.'

'At that rate,' said the Marquise, 'we may very well pretend to send influences to the Moon, and to give a judgement on their distempers. But since there is only requisite a little more wit and ingenuity in the inhabitants of that country, to blast the honour we flatter ourselves with, I confess, I am still a little apprehensive they may have some advantages over us.'

'Do not fear,' said I; 'there is no likelihood that we are the only fools in the universe. Ignorance is naturally a very general talent; and though I do but guess at that of the inhabitants of the Moon, yet I no more doubt of it, than I do of the most certain news we have from thence.'

'And what, pray, are these certain news you have from thence?' interrupted she.

'They are,' said I, 'Madam, such as are brought us every day by the learned, who travel daily thither by the help of long telescopes: they tell us they have discovered vast countries, seas, lakes, high mountains and deep valleys.'

'You surprise me,' said the Marquise. 'I know very well that mountains and valleys may be discovered in the Moon, by the remarkable inequality we see in its surface; but how do they distinguish countries and seas?'

'Very easily,' said I; 'because the water permits a part of the light to pass through it, and reflects less, and appears, at a great distance, to be obscure spots; and that the Earth, which is solid, reflects the whole light, and therefore must appear the brightest part of the globe on the Moon. These different parts are all so well known that they have given them all names of learned men: one place is called Copernicus; another, Archimedes; and a third, Galileo. There are too a Caspian Sea, Porphory Hills and the Black Lake. In short, they have framed so exact a description of the Moon, that a learned man, if he were there, would be in no more danger of losing his way, than I would be if I were at Paris.'

'But,' replied the Marquise, 'I should be very well pleased to have a further account of this country.'

''Tis impossible,' replied I, 'that the nicest observers should inform you so well as Astolpho, of whom you ought to enquire; and who was conducted to the Moon by St John. What I shall tell you now, is one of the most pleasant fooleries in all Ariosto; and I am satisfied, 'twill not displease you to know it. I own, I ought not to meddle with St John, whose name is so worthy of respect but since there is a poetical licence and liberty of conscience, it ought to pass as a gaiety. The whole poem is dedicated to a great churchman, and another great churchman has honoured it with signal approbation, which one may perceive by the several editions. See what he treats of.

'Orlando, nephew to Charlemagne, became mad because the fair Angelica had preferred Medora to him; one day Astolpho, the brave paladin, found himself in a terrestrial paradise, which was on the brink of a very high mountain whither his flying horse had carried him; there he met Saint John who told him that to cure the madness of Orlando 'twas necessary they should take a voyage to the Moon. Astolpho who desired nothing more than to see that country, wanted no entreaties, and behold on a sudden a chariot of fire carried the Saint and the paladin through the air. As Astolpho was no great philosopher, he was much surprised to see the Moon so vastly bigger than it appeared to him upon the Earth, and was much more amazed to see rivers, lakes, mountains, plains, groves, towns and forests, and (that which would have surprised me also) beautiful nymphs that hunted in those forests. But that which he beheld yet more rare, was a valley where he found all things that were lost on earth, of what kind soever, crowns, riches, renown, and grandeur, infinity of hopes, time lost in waiting and depending on promising statesmen, or thrown away at play; the alms that one causes to be given after one's death; the verses and dedications one presents to princes and the sighs of lovers.'

'As for the sighs of lovers,' replied the Marquise interrupting me, 'I know not whether in the time of Ariosto they were lost or not, but in ours I know of none that go into the Moon.'

'Were there none but you, Madam,' replied I, smiling, 'you have caused so many to sigh in vain that you have made a considerable treasure in the Moon: in short, the Moon is exact in collecting all that is lost here below, and which are all to be found there, even to the donation of Constantine. (But Ariosto told me this only in my ear.) Besides all the folly that was ever committed upon the earth is well preserved there; there are so many vials full of subtle and penetrating liquor, which easily evaporates as soon as opened, and upon every one of these vials is writ the name of those to whom it belongs. I believe that Ariosto put 'em all in one cup, but I had rather fancy myself that they were orderly placed in one gallery. Ariosto was very much astonished to see the vials of so many persons whom he believed to be very wise, and yet, notwithstanding, their vials were so very full; and for my part, I am persuaded that mine is as full as any since I entertain you with visions, both philosophic and poetical. That which comforts me is, that 'tis possible by what I am persuading you to believe, I shall very suddenly make you have a vial in the Moon as well as myself. The good paladin did not fail to find his own among the number, and by the permission of the saint, he took it and snuffed up the spirit as if it had been the Queen of Hungary's water. But Ariosto said he would not carry it far, and that it would return to the Moon again by a folly that he committed seven years after. But he did not forget the vial of Orlando which was the occasion of his voyage; he had a great deal of difficulty to carry it, for the spirit of this hero was in its own nature very heavy, and he did not want a drop of being full. But here Ariosto according to the laudable custom of speaking what he pleased, addressing himself to his mistress speaks to her thus in good verse:

That I ought to cause one to mount the heavens, my fair one, to make me recover the sense your charms have made me lose, yet I will not complain of this loss, provided it does not go too far, but if there be a necessity that your cruelties must continue, as they have begun, I have no more to do but to expect just such a fate as Orlando's; however I do not believe, that to recover my senses 'tis requisite I go through the air to the moon; my soul does not lodge so high; it wanders about your fair eyes and mouth; and if you will be pleased to give me leave to take it, permit me to recover it with my lips.

'Is not this witty for me to reason like Ariosto? I am of opinion that a man never loses his wits but for love; and you see they do not travel very far, while their lips only know so well how to recover 'em. But when one loses 'em by other means (as we lose 'em by philosophising) they go directly to the Moon, and one cannot retrieve 'em, when one pleases.'

'In recompense of this,' said the Marquise, 'our vials shall be honourable among the ranks of the philosophers: for our spirits will go on in wandering and erring on something that is worthy of 'em; but to accomplish this, and rid me of mine.

'But pray tell me seriously,' said the Marquise, 'do you believe that there are men in the Moon? For hitherto, you have said nothing to me as positively as to that.'

'I do not believe that there are men there, Madam, but some other odd sort of creatures. Pray, Madam, consider but how much the face of nature is changed betwixt this and China; other faces, other shapes, other manners, and almost quite different principles of reasoning, from this to the Moon the difference ought to be more considerable. When one travels towards the new discovered world of America, etc. and finds the inhabitants to be hardly men, but rather a kind of brutes in human shape, and that not perfect either, so that could we travel to the orb of the Moon, I do not think we should find men and women there.'

'What kind of creatures should we find then?' said the Marquise, with a very impatient look.

'I swear I cannot tell,' said I, 'Madam, were it possible for us to be rational creatures and yet not men, and that we inhabited the Moon, could it ever enter into our imagination, that there dwelt here below so extravagant an animal as that of mankind? Could we fancy to ourselves any living creatures with such foolish passions, and so wise reflections; of so small duration, and yet can see so vast a prospect beyond it; of so much knowledge in trifles, and so much ignorance of important things; so earnest for liberty, yet so inclined to servitude and slavery; so very desirous of happiness, and yet so uncapable of attaining it; it would require a great deal of wit and judgement in the inhabitants of the Moon, to find the reason and mystery of such an odd composition; for we that see one another daily, have not yet found out how we are made. It was said of old amongst the heathens that the gods when they made man were drunk with nectar, whom when they had considered when sober, they could not forbear laughing at the ridiculousness of their handiwork.'

'We are then secure enough,' said the Marquise, 'that the inhabitants of the Moon will never guess what we are, but I wish we could attain the knowledge of them; for I must confess it makes me uneasy to think there are inhabitants in the Moon, and yet I cannot so much as fancy what kind of creatures they are.'

'And why are you not as uneasy,' said I, 'upon the account of the inhabitants under and near the South Pole, which is altogether unknown to us? They and we are carried as it were on the same ship, they in the stern, and we in the head, and yet you see there is no communication between the stern and the head, and that those at the one end of the ship do not know what kind of people they are on the other, nor what they are doing, and yet you would know what passes in the Moon, in that other great ship sailing in the heavens at a vast distance from us.'

'Ah,' said the Marquise, 'I look upon the inhabitants under the South Pole, as a people known to us, because they are most certainly very like us; and that we may see them if we please to give ourselves the trouble; they will continue still where they are, and cannot run away from our knowledge; but we shall never know what these inhabitants of the Moon are; 'tis that that vexes me.'

'If I should answer you seriously,' said I, 'that we may one day know 'em, would you not laugh at me? Nay and I should deserve it: yet I could defend myself very well if I should say so; there is a certain ridiculous thought in my head, which has some shadow of likelihood, which satisfies me, though I do not know on what it is founded, it being so impertinent as it is; yet I will lay you what you will, that I will oblige you to believe against all reason that there may one day be a correspondence between the Earth and the Moon. Reflect a little, Madam, upon the state and condition of America, before it was discovered by Christopher Columbus; its inhabitants lived in a most profound ignorance, so far from the knowledge of sciences, that they were ignorant of the most simple and useful art. They went stark naked and could not imagine that men could be covered by skins of beasts; had no other arms but bows, and who look upon the sea as a vast space forbidden to mankind, joining, as they thought, to the sky; beyond which they saw nothing. 'Tis true after having spent several years with hollowing the root of a great tree with sharp flints, they ventured to go in this kind of boat, which was driven along the shore by the winds and the waves; but as this kind of vessel was very subject to be overset very often, they were necessitated to swim to catch their boat again; and indeed, they did swim for the most part, except when they were weary. If anybody had told them there was a navigation much more perfect than that they knew; and that by it, it was easy to cross that vast extent of water to any side, and in what manner we pleased, and that it was possible to stop and lie still in the midst of the sea, while the waves were in motion; that men could move fast or flow as they pleased; and that the sea, notwithstanding the vastness of its extent, was no hindrance to the commerce of the distant nations, provided that there were people on the other shore; surely the Indians would never have believed that man that should have told 'em this, to them, impossibility. Nevertheless, the day came that the strangest and least expected sight that they ever saw presented itself to their view, huge great bodies, which seemed to have white wings with which they flew upon the sea, belching fire from all parts, and at last landed upon their shore a race of unknown men, all crusted over with polished steel, ordering and disposing at their pleasure the monsters that brought them thither, carrying thunder in their hands which destroyed all that made any resistance, while the wondering Indians cried, "From whence came they?" "Who brought them over the seas?" "Who has given 'em the power of fire and thunder?" "Are they gods or the children of the sun? For certainly, they are not men." I know not, Madam, whether you conceive, as I do, the extraordinary surprise of these Americans, but certainly there was never any equal to it; and after that, I will not swear, but there may be one day a commerce betwixt the Earth and the Moon. Had the Americans any reason to hope for a correspondence betwixt America and Europe (which they did not know)? It is true there will be a necessity to cross the vast extent of air and heaven that is betwixt the Earth and the Moon. But did these Americans think the ocean more proper to be crossed, and passed through?'

'Sure,' said the Marquise, 'you are mad,' and looking earnestly on me.

'I do not deny it,' answered I.

'Nay,' said she, 'it is not sufficient to confess it, I will prove you to be mad. The Americans were so ignorant, that the possibility of making a way or passage through the vast ocean, could never enter their thoughts; but we that know so much, we easily find out that it would be no hard matter to pass through the air if we could support ourselves.'

'There are those men,' said I, 'who have found out more than a possibility of it; for they actually begin to fly a little, and several have made and fitted wings to themselves, and invented a way to give themselves motion, for supporting the body in the air, for crossing of rivers, and flying from one steeple to another. 'Tis true, these were not flights of an eagle; and it has cost some of these new birds a leg or an arm: but this essay is like the first planks that were carried on the water, which yet gave beginnings to shipping; and there was a very great difference between these planks and ships of mighty burden; yet you see that time by degrees has produced great ships. The art of flying is but in its infancy, time must bring it to maturity, and one day men will be able to fly to the Moon.'

'Do you pretend to have discovered all things,' said she, 'or to have brought them to that perfection that nothing can be added?'

'Pray, Madam,' said I, 'by consent, let us save something for the age to come.'

'I will never yield,' said she, 'that men will ever be able to fly without breaking their necks.'

'Well,' said I, 'Madam, since you will needs have men always to fly so ill, it may be the inhabitants of the Moon will fly better, and will be fitter for the trade; for 'tis all one, if we go to them or they to us. And we shall be like the Americans, who do not believe navigation possible, when at the same time, sailing was so well understood on the other half of the globe.'

'Sure,' said she, in anger, 'the inhabitants of the Moon would have been with us before now, if that were likely.'

'Pardon me,' said I, 'Madam, the Europeans did not sail to America till after six thousand years, all that time was requisite for performing navigation. The inhabitants of the Moon, it may be, at that time, knew how to make little journeys in the air, and are now practising; and it may be when they have more skill, we shall see 'em. And God knows what strange surprise 'twill be to us.'

'This is insupportable,' said the Marquise, 'to banter me on thus with such frivolous arguments.'

'If you anger me,' said I, 'I know what I have to say to enforce 'em and make all good. Observe, Madam, how the world is daily more and more unfolded. The ancients believed the torrid and the frozen zones uninhabitable for extremity of cold or heat; and the Romans confined the general map of the world to their own empire, which carried as much of grandeur as ignorance. But we know that there are inhabitants both in these extreme hot and extreme cold countries; by this the world is much augmented. Then it was believed that the ocean covered all the Earth, except what was inhabited; and that there was no antipodes; for the ancients never heard of them: besides they could not believe men would have their feet opposite to ours, with their heads hanging down; and yet after all this the antipodes are discovered, the map of the world is corrected, and a new half added to the world. You understand my meaning,' said I, 'Madam; these antipodes which have been discovered contrary to all expectation, ought to make us more circumspect in judging by appearances: the world and secrets of nature will be daily more and more discovered: and at last we may come to know somewhat more of the Moon.'

'Certainly,' said the Marquise, looking earnestly on me, 'I see you so charmed with this opinion that I doubt not but you believe all you say.'

'I should be very sorry to find myself so,' said I; 'my endeavour is only to show that chimerical opinion may be so far defended by strength of argument as to amuse a person of your understanding and sense, but not to persuade. Nothing but truth itself has that influence, even without ornaments of all its convincing proofs; it penetrates so naturally into the soul that one seems but to call it to mind; though it be the first time that ever one heard of it.'

'Now you ease me,' said she, 'for your false way of arguing did confound and incommode me, but now I can go sleep soundly; for, if you please, let us retire.'

My lady Marquise would needs engage me to pursue and continue our discourse by daylight; but I told her 'twas more proper to reserve our fancies and notions till the night; and since the Moon and stars were the subject of our conversation, to trust it only to them. We did not fail to go that evening into the park, which was now become a place consecrated to our philosophical entertainment.

'I have a great deal of news to tell you,' said I. 'The Moon, which I told you last night (by all appearance) was inhabited, now I begin to think, may be otherwise; for I have been reflecting upon a thing which puts its inhabitants in great danger.'

'I shall never suffer that,' said the Marquise, 'for you, having prepared me last night, put me in hopes to see these people arrive one day upon your Earth; and today, you will not allow them a being in the universe. You shall not impose upon me at this rate. You made me believe there were inhabitants in the Moon; I have overcome all the difficulties my reason suggested to me against that opinion, and now I am resolved I will believe it.'

'You go too fast,' said I, 'Madam; one ought to give but one half of one's thoughts and belief to opinions of this nature, reserving the other half free for receiving the contrary opinion, if there be occasion.'

'I am not to be deluded,' replied the Marquise, 'with fair words; let us come to the subject matter in debate: must not we reason the same way of the inhabitants of the Moon, as we did of your Saint-Denis?'

'Not at all, Madam,' answered I; 'the Moon does not so much resemble the Earth, as Saint-Denis does Paris. The Sun draws from the Earth waters, exhalations and vapours; which ascending into the air, to certain height, are gathered together, and form clouds; these clouds, hanging in the air, move irregularly round our globe and overshadow sometimes one country, sometimes another. And if it were possible for anyone to see and consider the Earth at a great distance, he would perceive great changes as to the appearance of its surface; for a great country, covered with clouds, would appear to be a very obscure part of the globe, and will become clear and enlightened as soon as these clouds disappear; and one would see these obscure places change their situation, meeting together in different figures, or disappearing altogether. We should see therefore the same changes upon the surface of the Moon, were it encompassed with clouds, as the Earth is; but on the contrary, all the obscurities, or dark places, as also those parts are enlightened, are still the same, fixed to the same situation, without variation or change; there lies the difficulty. And for this reason, the sun draws no vapours or exhalation from the globe of the Moon; and by consequence 'tis a body infinitely harder and more solid than our Earth, whose subtle parts are easily separated from the rest, and mount upward, being once set in motion by the heat of the Sun: so that the Moon must needs be nothing else but a vast heap of rocks and marble, from which no vapour can be exhaled; which vapours are so essential and natural to waters, that 'tis impossible the one can be without the other. Who can then be the inhabitants of those rocks that produce nothing? Or what living creatures can subsist in a country without water?'

'How!' cried my lady Marquise. 'Have you forgot that you assured me, there were seas in the Moon, which we could distinguish from hence?'

'That's only a conjecture,' said I, 'and I am very sorry that these obscure places, that may be taken for seas, are, possibly, nothing else but deep caverns, and vast cavities; and guessing is pardonable, at the great distance we are at from the Moon.'

'But,' said she, 'is that sufficient to make us reject the inhabitants of the Moon?'

'Not altogether, Madam,' said I, 'nor must we absolutely declare either for 'em, or against 'em.'

'I confess my weakness,' said she; 'I am not capable of such indifference, and I must be positive in my belief; therefore let us free ourselves of one opinion; let us either preserve the inhabitants of the Moon, or annihilate 'em forever, never to be heard of again; but, if possible, let us preserve 'em, for I have an inclination and a kindness for 'em, I would not willingly lose.'

'I shall not unpeople the Moon then, Madam,' said I, 'but for your sake shall restore to it its inhabitants. And the truth is that by the appearance of the obscure and enlightened places of the Moon, which are still the same, without change, we have no reason to believe that there are any clouds surrounding it, which might obscure sometimes one place, sometimes another; but yet that does not argue, but she may emit vapours and exhalations. Our clouds which we see carried in the air, are nothing but exhalations and vapours, which are separate in particles, too small to be seen; which meeting with cold airs, as they ascend, by it are condensed, and rendered visible to us, by the reunion of their parts; after which they become thick and black clouds, which float in the air, as stranger bodies, till at last they fall upon the Earth in rain. But sometimes it falls out that the same vapours and exhalations are extended, and kept from joining together and so are imperceptible, and are only gathered together so far as to form a kind of small dew, so very subtle that it cannot be seen as 'tis a-falling. It may be, in like manner, that the vapours which proceed from the Moon (for certainly it emits vapours) and 'tis impossible to believe that the Moon can be such a body, as that all its parts should be of equal solidity, and so equal a temper, one with the other, that they are incapable of receiving any change, by the attracting and moving influence of the Sun upon 'em: we know no body of this nature, the hardest marbles are not of this kind; and there is no body, how hard and solid soever, but is subject to change and alteration, either by secret and invincible motion in itself, or by some exterior impulse it removed from another. It may be therefore, as I said, the vapours which arise from the Moon are not gathered together, as around her, into clouds, but fall gently upon it again in insensible dews, and not in rain: and 'tis sufficient to demonstrate this, to conjecture only, that the air which environs the Moon, is as different from the air that environs the Earth, as the vapours of the one from the exhalations of the other; which is more than likely to be true; and it must follow that matter being otherwise disposed of in the Moon, than in the Earth, its effects should also be different; and imports nothing, whether it be an interior motion of the parts of the Moon, or the production of external causes, which furnish it with inhabitants, and them with sufficient food for their subsistence; so that, in our imagination, we may furnish 'em with fruits and grain of several sorts, waters, and what else we please; for fruits, grain and water, I understand, are agreeable to the nature of the Moon, of whose nature I know nothing; and all these proportioned and fitted to the necessities of the inhabitants, of whom I know as little.'

'That is to say,' said the Marquise, 'that you only know that all is very well there, without knowing in what manner; that is a great deal of ignorance, with a little knowledge, but we must have patience. However I think myself very happy, you have restored the Moon its inhabitants again; and I am very much pleased, you have surrounded it with air of its own, for without that, I should think a planet too naked.'

'These different airs,' answered I, 'hinder the communication and commerce of these two planets. If flying would do the business, what do I know, but we might come to perfection in that art I discoursed of last night. I confess, Madam, there seems but little likelihood of what I say, since the great distance between the Moon and the Earth makes the difficulty so hard to overcome, which is very considerable; but though it were not, and that the Earth and the Moon were placed near one another, yet it would not be possible to pass from the air of the Earth, to the air of the Moon. The water is the air and element of fish, who never pass into the air and element of birds; 'tis not the distance that hinders 'em, but 'tis because everyone of 'em are confined to the air which they breathe. We find that our air is mixed with vapours that are thicker and grosser than those of the Moon; and, by consequence, any inhabitants of the Moon who should arrive upon the confines of our world, would be drowned and suffocated as soon as they entered into our air, and we should see 'em fall dead upon the earth.'

'Oh, but I should be glad,' cried the Marquise, 'that some great shipwreck, occasioned by a mighty tempest, would throw a good many of these people upon our world, that we might at leisure consider their extraordinary shape and figure.'

'But,' answered I, 'if they had skill enough to sail upon the external surface of our air, and that from thence they should catch us, like fish, out of curiosity of seeing us; would that please you, Madam?'

'Why not?' said she, laughing. 'I would go of myself into their nets to have the satisfaction of seeing those that had caught me.'

'Consider,' said I, 'that you would be very weak and feeble, before you come to the surface of our air, for we cannot breathe it in all its extent, and we can hardly live on the tops of high mountains; and I wonder that those who are so foolish as to believe that corporeal geniuses inhabit the purest air do not tell us why these geniuses visit us so seldom, and stay so short a while: I do believe 'tis because few amongst 'em know how to dive; and that even those who are skilful in that art have great difficulty to penetrate the grossness of the air which we breathe. You see therefore that nature has set many bars and fences, to hinder us from going out of our world, into that of the Moon. However, for our satisfaction, let us conjecture and guess as much as we can of that world: for example, I fancy that the inhabitants of the Moon must see the heavens, the Sun, and the stars of a different colour than what they appear to us. All these objects we see through a kind of natural perspective-glass, which changes them to us; this perspective-glass of ours is mixed with vapours and exhalations, which do not ascend very high. Some of late pretend that the air of itself is blue, as well as the water of the sea; and that that colour is not apparent in the one, nor the other, but at a great depth. The heavens, say they, in which are placed the fixed stars has of itself no light; and by consequence ought to appear black: but we see it through our air, which is blue; and therefore the heavens appear of that colour. If it be so, the beams of the sun and stars cannot pass through the air without taking a little of its tincture, and at the same time lose as much of their own natural colour. But supposing the air had no colour of itself, 'tis certain that a flambeau seen at a distance, through a thick fog, appears of a reddish colour, tho' that be not natural to it; so all our air, which is nothing else but a thick fog, must certainly alter the true natural colour of the heavens, Sun and stars to us; for nothing but the pure heavenly substance is capable to convey to us light and colours, in their purity and perfection, as they are: so that the air of the Moon is of another nature than our air, or is, of itself, of an indifferent colour; or, at least, is another fog, changing, in appearance, the colours of the celestial bodies. In short, if there be inhabitants in the Moon they see all things changed, through their perspective-glasses, which is their air.'

'That makes me prefer our place of habitation,' said the Marquise, 'to that of the Moon, for I cannot believe, that the mixture of the heavenly colours is so fine there, as it is here. Let us suppose, if you will, the heavens of a reddish colour, and the stars of a greenish, the effect would not be half so agreeable as stars of gold, upon a deep blue.'

'To hear you speak,' said I, 'one would think you were fitting of furniture for a room, or choosing a garniture for a suit of clothes. Believe me, nature is very ingenious, therefore let us leave to her care the finding out a mixture of colours agreeable to the inhabitants of the Moon; and I assure you, 'twill be perfectly well understood; she certainly has not failed of changing the scene of the universe according to the different situation and position of the beholders, and still in a new and agreeable way.'

'I know the skill of nature perfectly well,' said Madam the Marquise; 'and she has spared herself the pains of changing her objects, as to the several points from whence they may be seen, and has only changed the perspective-glasses through which they are seen; and has the honour of this great variety, without the expense: she has bestowed on us a blue heaven, with a blue air; and it may be, she has bestowed upon the inhabitants of the Moon, a heaven of scarlet, with an air of the same colour, and yet their heaven and ours is one and the same. And it seems to me that nature has given every one of us a perspective-glass, or tube, through which we behold objects in a very different manner, one from the other. Alexander the Great saw the Earth as a fine place, fit for him to form a great empire upon; Celadon only looked upon it as a dwelling-place of Astraea; a philosopher considers it as a great planet, all covered over with fools, moving through the heavens; and I do not see that the object changes more from the Earth to the Moon, than it does here from one man to another.'

'The change of sights is more surprising to our imagination,' said I; 'for they are still the same objects we see at different views; and it may be, in the Moon they see other objects than we see; at least, they do not see a part of those we see. Perhaps in that country they know nothing of the dawning of the day, of the twilight before sun-rising, and after sun-setting; for the beams of the Sun, at these two times, being oblique and faint, do not have strength to penetrate the grossness and thickness of the air with which we are environed; but are received and intercepted by the air, before they can fall upon the Earth, and are reflected upon us by the air; so that daybreak and twilight are favours of nature which we enjoy by the by, or, as it were, by chance, they not having been destined for us; but 'tis likely that the air of the Moon, being purer than ours, is not so proper and fit for reflecting the faint beams of the Sun before its rising, and after its setting; therefore I suppose, the inhabitants of the Moon do not enjoy the favourable light of the aurora, or dawning, which growing stronger and stronger does prepare us for the glorious appearance of the Sun at noon; nor the twilight, which becoming more faint by degrees, we are insensibly accustomed to the absence of the Sun. So that the inhabitants of the Moon are in profound darkness, when on a sudden a curtain is drawn, as it were, and their eyes are dazzled with the rays of the Sun, and they enjoy a bright resplendent light; when by a sudden motion, as quick as the former, down falls the curtain, and instantly they are reduced to their former darkness. They want those mediums, or instices, which join day and night together (and which participate of both) which we enjoy. Besides, these people have no rainbow; for as the dawning is an effect of the thickness of our air, so the rainbow is formed upon exhalations and vapours, condensed into black clouds, which pour down rain upon us by diverse reflections and refractions of the sunbeams upon these clouds: so that we owe the obligation of the most agreeable and pleasant effects, to the ugliest and most disagreeable causes in nature. And since the purity of the air of the Moon deprives it of clouds, vapours and rain, adieu to rainbow and aurora: to what then can the lovers in the Moon compare their mistresses, without these two things?'

'I do not much regret that loss,' said the Marquise, 'for in my opinion, the inhabitants of the Moon are fully recompensed for the want of rainbow, daybreak and twilight, since for the same reason, they have neither thunder nor lightning, both of which are produced by clouds and exhalations; they enjoy bright serene days, and never lose the Sun by day, nor the stars by night. They know nothing of storms and tempest; which seem to us the effects of the wrath of heaven. And can you think their condition is so much to be lamented?'

'You,' said I, 'Madam, represent the Moon as a most charming abode. Now methinks it should not be so desirous and agreeable to have a burning sun always over one's head, without the interpolation of any clouds to moderate its heat: and it may be for this reason, nature has sunk these caverns in the Moon, which are big enough to be seen by our telescopes. Who knows but the inhabitants of the Moon retire to these cavities, when they are incommoded with the excessive heat of the Sun, and it may be they live nowhere else, but build their towns and villages in these hollow places? And do we not know that Rome which is built underground is almost as great as the city above ground? So that if we should suppose that the city of Rome above ground should be razed and quite removed, Rome underground would then be just such a town as those have imagined to be in the Moon. Whole nations live in these vast caverns and I doubt not but there may be passages underground for the communication and commerce of one people and nation with another. You are pleased to laugh, Madam, at my fancy, do so with all my heart, I agree you should; and yet you may be more mistaken than I: for you believe that the inhabitants of the Moon dwell upon the surface of their globes, as we do on that of the Earth; it is very likely that 'tis just the contrary; for there is most certain a vast difference between their way of living and ours.'

'No matter,' said the Marquise, 'I cannot resolve to suffer the inhabitants of the Moon to live in perpetual darkness.'

'You would be harder put to it, Madam,' said I, 'if you knew that a great philosopher of old, believed the Moon to be the abode and dwelling of the souls who had merited happiness by their good life in this world, and that their felicity consisted in hearing the harmony of the spheres as they turned round, and that they were deprived of this heavenly music as often as the Moon was obscured by the shadows of the Earth; and that then these souls roared and cried out as in despair, and that the Moon made haste to recover her light again to bring the souls out of that affliction.'

'At that rate,' said she, 'we should see the blessed souls come from the Moon to us; for why should not the Earth be to the Moon, as the Moon is to the Earth, since according to the opinion of your philosopher, there was no other felicity for the souls of the blessed, than to be transported from one world to the other?'

'Seriously,' said I, 'Madam, 'twould be a great pleasure and satisfaction to see several different worlds; and I am often glad to make these journeys in imagination; what joy then it would be to do it in reality; that would be far better than to travel hence to Japan, crawling as it were with difficulty from one point of this globe to another, and still to see nothing but men and women over and over again.'

'Well,' said she, 'what hinders but we should make a journey through the planets as well as we can? Let us by imagination place ourselves in several positions, and situations, for considering the universe. Have we no more to see in the Moon?'

'No,' said I, 'at least, I have shown you all I know. Going out of the Moon towards the Sun, the first planet you meet with is Venus; and here I must again make use of my former simile of Paris and Saint-Denis. Venus turns round the Sun on her own axis, as the Moon does round the Earth; and by the means of telescopes, we discover that Venus waxes and wanes, being sometimes altogether enlightened, and sometimes darkened according to her different positions in respect to the Earth. By all appearance the Moon is inhabited, why should not Venus be so, as well as she?'

'Ay, but –,' interrupted the Marquise, 'by your "why nots" you will people all the planets.'

'Do not doubt of it, Madam,' answered I; 'why has not nature sufficient to give inhabitants to 'em all? We see that all the planets are of the same nature, that they are all opaque solid bodies, having no light but what they receive from the Sun; which they send one to another by reflection, and that they have all the same kind of motion; thus far equal, and after all this must we conceive that all these vast bodies were made not to be inhabited? And that nature has made only an exception in favour of the Earth, he that will believe this, may, but for my part I cannot.'

'I find you,' said the Marquise, 'very resolute and settled in your opinion of a sudden: a little while ago, you would scarce allow the Moon to be inhabited; and seemed to be very indifferent, whether it were so or not; whereas now, I am confident you would be very angry with anybody that should tell you that all the planets were not inhabited.'

'It is true, Madam, in the minute wherein you have surprised me, had you contradicted me, as to the inhabitants of all the planets, I would not only have defended my opinion, but have proceeded to have given you an exact description of all the several inhabitants of the planets. There are certain moments of believing things; and I never so firmly believed the planets to be inhabited, as in that moment I spoke of 'em; but now, after cooler thoughts, I should think it very strange, that the Earth should be inhabited as it is; and that other planets should be so entirely desolate and deserted: for you must not think, that we see all the living creatures that inhabit the Earth. For there are as many several species and kinds of animals invisible, as there are visible. We see distinctly from the elephant to the mite; there our sight is bounded and there are infinite numbers of living creatures lesser than a mite, to whom, a mite is as big in proportion, as an elephant is to it. The late invention of glasses called microscopes, have discovered thousands of small living creatures, in certain liquors, which we could never have imagined to be there. And it may be the different tastes of these liquors, proceed from these little animals who bite and sting our tongues and palates. If you mix certain ingredients in these liquors (as pepper in water) and expose 'em to the heat of the Sun, or let 'em putrefy you shall see other new species or living creatures. Several bodies, which appear to be solid, are nothing else but collections or little heaps of these imperceptible animals who find there as much room as is required for them to move in. The leaf of a tree is a little world inhabited by such invisible little worms: to them this leaf seems of a vast extent, they find hills and valleys upon it. And there is no more communication between the living creatures on the one side, and those on the other, than between us and the antipodes. And I think there is more reason to believe a planet (which is so vast a body) to be inhabited. There has been found in several sorts of very hard stones infinite multitudes of little worms, lodged all over them in insensible vacuities; and who are nourished upon the substance of these stones which they eat. Consider the vast numbers of these little animals, and how long a tract of years they have lived upon a grain of sand. And by this argument, though my Moon were nothing but a confused heap of marble rocks, I would rather make it be devoured and consumed by its inhabitants, than to place none at all in it.

'To conclude, everything lives and everything is animate; that is to say, if you comprehend the animals that are generally known, the living creatures latterly discovered and those that will be discovered hereafter, you will find that the Earth is very well peopled and that nature has been so liberal in bestowing them, that she has not been at the pains to discover half of 'em. After this, can you believe that nature, who has been fruitful to excess as to the Earth, is barren to all the rest of the planets?'

'My reason is convinced,' said the Marquise, 'but my fancy is confounded with the infinite number of living creatures that are in the planets; and my thoughts are strangely embarrassed with the variety that one must of necessity imagine to be amongst 'em; because I know nature does not love repetitions; and therefore they must all be different. But how is it possible for one to represent all these to our fancy?'

'Our imaginations can never comprehend this variety,' said I, 'let us be satisfied with our eyes, or we may easily conceive by an universal view, nature has formed variety in the several worlds. All the faces of mankind are in general the same form. Yet the two great nations of our globe, the Europeans and Africans, seem to have been made after different models. Nay, there is a certain resemblance and air of the countenance peculiar to every family or race of men. Yet it is wonderful to observe how many millions of times nature has varied so simple a thing as the face of a man. We, the inhabitants of the Earth, are but one little family of the universe, we resemble one another. The inhabitants of another planet are another family, whose faces have another air peculiar to themselves; by all appearance, the difference increases with the distance, for could one see an inhabitant of the Earth and one of the Moon together, he would perceive less difference between them than between an inhabitant of the Earth, and one of Saturn. Here (for example) we have the use of the tongue and voice and in another planet, it may be, they only speak by signs. In another, the inhabitants speak not at all. Here our reason is formed and made perfect by experience. In another place, experience adds little or nothing to reason. Further off, the old know no more than the young. Here we trouble ourselves more to know what's to come, than to know what's passed. In another planet, they neither afflict themselves with the one nor the other; and 'tis likely they are not the less happy for that. Some say we want a sixth sense by which we should know a great many things we are now ignorant of. It may be the inhabitants of some other planet have this advantage; but want some of those other five we enjoy; it may be also that there are a great many more natural senses in other worlds; but we are satisfied with the five that are fallen to our share, because we know no better. Our knowledge is bounded to certain limits, which the wit of man could never yet exceed. There is a certain point where our ingenuity is at a stand; that which is beyond it is for some other world, where it may be some things, that are familiar to us, are altogether unknown. Our globe enjoys the pleasure of love; but is destroyed in several places by the fury of war. Another planet enjoys constant peace, without the delights of love, which must render their lives very irksome. In fine, nature has done to the several worlds in great, as she has done to us mortals in little by making some happy, others miserable. Yet she has never forgot her admirable art in varying all things, though she has made some equal in some respects, by compensating the want of any one thing, with another of equal value.

'Are you satisfied,' said I, 'Madam, very gravely; have I not told you chimeras in abundance? Truly, I find not so much difficulty to comprehend these differences of worlds; my imagination is working upon the model you have given me; and I am representing to my own mind odd characters and customs for these inhabitants of the other planets. Nay more, I am forming extravagant shapes and figures for 'em: I can describe 'em to you; for I fancy I see 'em here. I leave these shapes,' said I, 'Madam, to entertain you in dreams this night; tomorrow, we shall know, if they have afflicted you, to describe the inhabitants of some other planet.'

THE FOURTH NIGHT

The dreams of my lady Marquise were not lucky, they still represented to her something like what we see on Earth; so that I had as much reason to reproach her, as certain people have to blame us when they see some of our pictures; for they being ignorant of drawing, and designing, and pleasing themselves with their extravagant and grotesque figures, tell us, our pictures are nothing but men and women, and there is no fancy in 'em. There was therefore no necessity of laying aside all sorts of the forms and figure of those animals that inhabit several planets, and to rest satisfied by guessing as well as we can, in pursuing our journey, which we had begun, through the several worlds of the universe.

'We were at Venus and there is no doubt,' said I to my lady Marquise, 'but Venus turns upon her own axis, but 'tis not known in what time, and by consequence, we know not the length of her days, but her years must consist but of eight months, since Venus turns round the Sun in that space of time. As Venus is forty times less than the Earth, the Earth must necessarily appear to the inhabitants of Venus, to be forty times bigger than Venus appears to us; and as the Moon is also forty times less than the Earth, by consequence, it must appear to the inhabitants of Venus, about the same bigness that Venus appears to us.'

'You afflict me,' said the Marquise, 'extremely; I see very well, that our Earth is not that happy planet to the inhabitants of Venus, as she is to us; or our globe of the Earth must appear too big to the inhabitants of Venus, to be a fountain of love, but the Moon, which appears to the world of Venus, of the same size that Venus appears to us, is exactly cut out to the source of their amours, and the lucky star of their intrigues; which titles are most agreeable to the pretty, clear, twinkling planets, which have in 'em a certain air of gallantry. 'Tis certainly a happy fate for our Moon to give laws to the loves of the inhabitants of Venus: no doubt, but these people are very soft, and have the art to please extremely well.'

'Without dispute, Madam,' said I, 'the very mobile of Venus are all made up of Celadons and Silvanders, and their most ordinary conversations excel the finest in Clelia; the climate, being nearer the sun than we, receives from its influence a brighter light and a more enlivening heat.'

'I perceive very well,' interrupted the Marquise, 'what kind of people the inhabitants of Venus are; they are, like our Moors of Granada, a sort of little sunburnt gentlemen, always in love, full of life and fire, given to making verses, and great lovers of music, and every day inventing feasts, balls and masquerades, to entertain their mistresses.'

'Pray, Madam,' said I, 'you are very ill acquainted with the inhabitants of Venus; for our Moors of Granada are, in respect to them, as the inhabitants of Lapland, or Greenland, for coldness and stupidity.

'But what then must the inhabitants of Mercury be, for they are yet more near to the Sun? They must certainly be mad, by having too much light and fire; and I believe they have no more memory than the most part of our Negroes; they never think and are void of all reflection, and they only act by chance and by sudden impulses. In short, the planet Mercury must certainly be the Bethlehem of the universe; they see the Sun a great deal bigger than we do, because they are so much nearer to it; he darts upon 'em so strong a light that if the inhabitants of Venus were here they would take our finest days for the remains of a faint twilight; and it may be the light we enjoy would not serve them to distinguish one object from another; and the heat they are accustomed to is so excessive that the greatest warmth enjoyed by the inhabitants of the middle of Africa would freeze them to death. Their year lasts but three months; the length of their day is yet unknown, Mercury being so little a planet and so near to the Sun, in whose rays he is so occasionally lost, that he is hitherto scarce discoverable by the art and skills of astronomers, who would never yet get so much hold of Mercury as to observe the time in which he performs his revolutions upon his own axis or centre; but the smallness of his planets persuades me 'tis a very short time, and then, by consequence, his days are very short and his inhabitants must see the Sun as a very great flaming brazier, very near their heads, which, to their apprehension, moves with wonderful rapidity; this makes them so earnestly wish for the coming nights, which, no doubt, must be much more grateful to 'em than the day; and during those cooler hours, they are enlightened by Venus, and by the Earth; which two planets must appear to them of considerable bigness. As for the other planets, since they are removed further than Mercury towards the firmament, his inhabitants must see them less than they appear to us, and receive but little light from 'em, it may be none at all, the fixed stars must appear less to them also, and they lose the light of some of 'em entirely, which, in my opinion, is a very great loss; for I should be very sorry to see the vast arched roof of the heavens adorned with fewer stars, or those I do see, appear less, and not so bright.'

'I am not so much concerned for that loss,' said the Marquise, 'as for their being so extremely incommoded with excessive heat; and I wish with all my heart, we could ease 'em of that trouble. Let us therefore allow 'em long and continued rain, to refresh 'em; such as are in some of the hot countries of our earth, which fall for four months together, during the hottest seasons.'

'That may be done,' said I; 'but we may find out another remedy to relieve the inhabitants of Mercury; for there are countries in China which, by their situation, must be very hot; yet notwithstanding, the cold is so excessive during the months of July and August that the rivers are frozen. The reason is, these climates abound with saltpetre (whose exhalations being very cold) the force of the heat draws out of the Earth in great abundance. Let us therefore suppose Mercury to be a little planet, made of saltpetre; and let the Sun extract out of himself a remedy to his disease which he gives to the inhabitants. This is certain, that nature produces no animal but in places where they may live; and customs and use, joined with ignorance of what is better, supplieth all defects and makes life agreeable; for ought we know, the inhabitants of Mercury want neither rain, nor exhalations of saltpetre.

'After Mercury, you know, the next planet we find in our journey, is the Sun; and if we judge by the Earth (which is inhabited) that other bodies of the same kind may be so too, we are mistaken, and the "why not" will fail us here; for the Sun is a body of a quite different nature from the Earth and other planets: he is the source and fountain of all that light, which the other planets do only reflect from one to another, after having received it from him; and so they can exchange light one with another, but are incapable of producing it. The Sun alone draws itself this precious substance which he darts around him with great force and violence, and which is intercepted by every body that is solid; so that there is reflected from one planet to another long streams and streaks of light, which, crossing and traversing each other in the air, are interwoven a thousand different ways and so form a mixture of the richest substance in nature. For this end the Sun is placed in the centre, which is the situation most proper and commode; from whence he may equally dispense and distribute his light and heat, for the livening and enlightening all things round him. The Sun is therefore a body of a particular substance; but what kind of body, or what kind of substance, is all the difficulty. Heretofore 'twas believed that the Sun was pure fire; but the error of this opinion was found out in the beginning of this age, by spots which were discovered upon the surface of the Sun; as a little after that time, there were new planets discovered, of which I shall speak hereafter. The learned part of the world were full of nothing else but these new planets; and discourses of 'em were so much in fashion that they believed the spots in the Sun were nothing else but these new planets, moving round 'em, which necessarily hid a part of his body from our sight, when their obscure side was turned towards us. The learned men of the world made their court to most kings and princes with these new discovered planets; giving the name of one prince to one, and of another prince to another; so that they were like to quarrel, to whom they should belong.'

'I am not pleased with that at all,' said the Marquise. 'You told me the other night that the philosophers and learned men had given the names of philosophers, astronomers and mathematicians to the several countries of the Moon, and I was very well satisfied, and think it but just that since the kings and princes possess the Earth, that they ought to suffer philosophers and astronomers to rule in the Moon and the stars, without encroaching upon 'em?'

'What,' said I, 'Madam, will not you allow kings and princes some corner of the Moon, or some star, to take their part in time of need? As to the spots in the Sun, they can be of no manner of use to 'em; for it has been found they are not planets, but clouds of smoke and vapours, and, as it were, a scum arising from the surface of the Sun; for sometimes they appear in great quantities, sometimes in less, and at other times they disappear; sometimes they join in one, and other times they are dispersed and dissipated; so that it should seem, the Sun is a liquid substance; some say 'tis of melted gold, which boils incessantly, and produces those impurities; and by the force of its motion, throws upon the surface its scum and dross; and as those consume, new ones are produced. Pray, Madam, fancy to yourself what strange bodies these spots of the Sun must be; there are some of 'em full as big as the globe of the Earth; judge then what a great quantity there must be of this melted gold, and of the extent of this vast ocean of light and fire, which we call the Sun. They say the Sun appears, through telescopes, to be full of great mountains which vomit flames, and that there is, as it were, a million of Mount Etnas joined together; but at the same time they acknowledge that these mountains may be altogether visionary, and that they are nothing else but the efects of the glasses of the telescopes. To whom shall we trust then when these very glasses, to which we owe so many new discoveries, deceive us? In fine, let the Sun be what it will, it does not at all seem proper to be inhabited; and yet 'tis pity, for the situation would be extremely fine; its inhabitants would be placed in the centre of the universe, and would see all the other planets turn regularly round 'em, whereas we observe infinite irregularities in their course; and 'tis only because we are not in a proper situation to consider 'em, as not being in the centre of their motion. Is it not hard that there is but one place in the universe, where the study of the stars would be easy, and that that place alone should be uninhabitable?'

'You do not think whilst you speak,' said the Marquise, 'were any living creatures in the Sun, he would see neither planets, nor fixed stars; nor, indeed, anything; the brightness of the Sun would render all things else invisible; and if there were inhabitants in the Sun, they would be apt to believe themselves the only people in nature.'

'I confess,' said I, 'I am mistaken, I considered only the situation of the Sun, without the effects of its light. But pray, Madam, allow me to tell you, that you, who have corrected me so justly, may also be mistaken yourself: the inhabitants of the Sun would not so much see itself; for they would be incapable to support the dazzling of his light, or unable to receive it, by being too near; and all things well considered, the Sun would be a country of blind men only. So that, once for all, I conclude, the Sun cannot be inhabited; and if you please, Madam, we will continue our journey to the other worlds. We are now come to the centre which is lowest point in all circular figures; and therefore must return back again and go upwards. In the way, we shall find Mercury, Venus, the Earth, and the Moon; all which planets we have visited.

'The next that presents itself to our observation is Mars, who contains nothing rare or curious that I know of: his days are not a full hour longer than ours, but his years are double the length of ours. Mars is less than the Earth, and his inhabitants see the Sun neither so big, nor so bright as we do. In short, Mars is not worthy the pains of a longer discourse; but 'tis very curious to observe Jupiter and his four moons, or guards: they are four little planets, which turn round Jupiter, as our Moon turns round us.'

'But,' says the Marquise, interrupting me, 'why are there some planets attending upon others, who, it may be, are no better than themselves? In my opinion, it would be more regular and uniform if all the planets, great and small, had but one motion round the Sun.'

'Ah, Madam!' said I, 'if you understood the tourbillions, or whirlings of Monsieur Descartes, whose name is so terrible and ideas so agreeable, you would not talk at that rate.'

'Let my brains turn round,' said she, laughing, 'if they will; I long to know what these tourbillions are; make haste therefore to satisfy me, I'll manage myself no longer but henceforth abandon all my thoughts to philosophy, without reserve, let the world talk what they please; but let me understand these whirlings.'

'I did not think you capable of such transports,' said I, 'Madam; and I am sorry they have not fitter object. But to satisfy you, a tourbillion is a heap of matter, whose parts are disjoined one from another, yet moving round all one way; each little part being allowed a particular motion of its own, provided always they do not obstruct the general circular motion. As for example, a tourbillion of air, called a whirlwind, or a hurricane, is an infinite quantity of little particles of air, turning all round together, carrying along everything they meet with in their way. You know that the planets are carried round in the celestial matter, which is incredibly subtle and swift; all that vast ocean, and mass of celestial substance, which is between the Sun, and the sphere of the fixed stars, turns round and carries with it the planets one way, from east and west, round the Sun, which is placed in the centre; but in shorter or longer time, as they are distant or nearer the centre, all things turn round, even the Sun itself, but he turns round upon his own axis. And you are to observe thus: if the Earth were in the middle of the celestial matter, as the Sun is, she would also turn round upon her own axis, like that. This is that great tourbillion, of which the Sun is, as it were, governor; but at the same time, all the planets have little whirlings peculiar to themselves, in imitation of the great one, the Sun; notwithstanding, they are all carried round the Sun, yet every one of them turns round upon his own axis, and sweeps along with him a share of the celestial substance which yields easily to any impulse of motion it receives, provided that does not obstruct its general motion round the Sun; and this is called the particular whirling or tourbillion of a planet, which extends as far as the sphere of its activity can reach; and if it fall so out that any lesser planet than that which governs the tourbillion comes in its way 'tis carried with it, and indispensably forced round it; but yet that does not hinder both the great planet, and the lesser, with their whirlings, to turn round with the great tourbillion of the Sun. 'Twas thus that, after the creation of the universe, the Earth carried the Moon round itself, because the Moon fell within the extent of its sphere of activity, and forced its obedience. Jupiter, of whom I have said somewhat already, was happier or stronger than we; there fell four little planets in his neighbourhood, and he subdued 'em all four. Our Earth, which is now a chief planet, had it fallen within the tourbillion of Jupiter, you may easily believe he would have forced us to have turned round him also, Jupiter being ninety times bigger than our Earth; and then we had been nothing but a moon depending upon Jupiter, whereas now the Earth has a moon of her own turning round her; so true it is that chance of situation has decided our fortune.'

'Pray, what assurance have we,' said the Marquise, 'that our Earth shall remain in the same situation? I am afraid we may make a trip one day or other, towards some planet as dangerous as Jupiter, who may sweep us round with itself; or that some other stronger planet may approach nearer to us; for I fancy that the violent motions of the heavenly matter you speak of may agitate and shake the planets so irregularly, that it might sometimes bring 'em nearer together, and at other times remove 'em further from one another.'

'We might gain rather than lose by that bargain,' said I; 'for it may be, our Earth would be carried near Venus and Mercury, which are little planets, and could not resist ours. But we have nothing either to hope or fear from such an accident; the planets must remain where they are, new conquests are forbid them, as they were heretofore to the kings of China. You know very well when one mixes oil and water together in a vessel, the oil will swim above; and if you throw any very light thing into the vessel, the oil will support it, and it will not penetrate into the water: throw in any other thing, somewhat heavier, of a proportionable weight to penetrate the oil, which is too weak to stop it; 'twill fall upon the water, and swim, the water being sufficiently strong to bear it up. So that this vessel, full of two liquors, which does not mingle together two bodies of an unequal weight, rests naturally in two different positions, the one above the other; so as the lightest can never descend, the heaviest can never ascend. If you add other liquors that will not mingle together, and throw as many bodies into 'em of proportionable weight, 'twill still be the same thing. Imagine to yourself, that the celestial substance which fills the vast tourbillion, or whirling of the Sun, is composed of different coats, wrapped within one another, like an onion; these coats are of different weights and force, as oil and water, and other liquors. The planets also are different weights; and by consequence, every one of the planets must stop upon that coat proportionable to its weight, and which has necessary strength for supporting it, and keeping it in an equal balance; and you will perceive it is not possible in nature they can remove from thence.'

'I understand very well,' said the Marquise, 'how these different weights are regulated, according to their several degrees. Would to God, there were some such order amongst us mortals to confine every man to the station that is fit for him.

I am now no longer in fear of Jupiter; I am satisfied that he will leave us at ease in our own little whirling, or tourbillion; I am easily pleased, and do not envy Jupiter his four moons.'

'You would be to blame if you should,' said I; 'for he has no more than what is necessary for him; considering the great distance he is from the Sun, his moons receive and reflect but a very faint light. 'Tis true, that Jupiter turns upon his own axis in the space of ten hours, his nights are but four hours long; and being so short, one would think he had no great need of four moons, but you must consider, in our Earth, under the North and South Poles, there are six months of day, and six months of night; because the two Poles being the two points of the Earth remotest from those countries and places, upon which the Sun darts his beams directly, and over which, to our apprehensions, he seems to perform his course. The Moon holds, or appears to us to hold, the same road with the Sun: so that if the inhabitants near the South and North Poles see the Sun during one half of his yearly course, and then lose his light during the other half, it must follow that they see the Moon during one half of her monthly revolution, and lose her during the other half; that is, for the space of fifteen days. One of Jupiter's years is twelve of ours, and there must be two opposite poles in that planet where there are days and nights of six years long apiece. A night of six years long is very long, and I believe these four moons were chiefly created for that reason. The highest of the four, as to Jupiter, performs its course round him in seventeen days, the second in seven days, the third in three days and a half, and the fourth in forty hours. These revolutions being thus divided by equal halves in these unhappy climates, where there are six years of continued night, one and twenty hours cannot pass without their seeing appear, at least, the last of the four moons; which is a very great satisfaction during so long and irksome a darkness. But upon whatever place of Jupiter you should inhabit, these four moons would represent to your view one of the most agreeable sights in nature: sometimes they rise all four together, then they separate according to the inequality of their motions; sometimes they see 'em over their heads, directly above one another; at other times they see 'em appear above their horizon, at equal distances; at another time, two of the four are rising, when the other two are setting; but above all, I should be pleased to see their constant eclipsing one another, or the Sun; for there passes no day without one of the two; and since eclipses are so familiar to that world, they must certainly be a divertissement to them, whereas they frighten the inhabitants of our Earth.'

'And you will not fail, I hope,' says the Marquise, 'to bestow inhabitants upon these four moons, though they be little, inferior planets, and only made to enlighten the inhabitants of a greater, during their long nights.'

'You need not doubt of it,' said I, 'Madam; these four planets are no less deserving of inhabitants, because they are so unhappy as to be subject to, and turn round, a more important planet.'

'I would,' said the Marquise, 'have the inhabitants of these four moons to be colonies of Jupiter, and receive their laws and manners from thence, and pay homage and respect to Jupiter, and not to look upon that great planet, but with veneration.'

'And would you not also,' said I, 'have these four moons to send ambassadors, from time to time, to the inhabitants of Jupiter, and swear fealty to him? For my part, we having no authority over the inhabitants of our Moon, makes me think that Jupiter has no more over the inhabitants of his four; and I believe, one of the advantages he has most reason to brag of, is that he frightens 'em. For example; the inhabitants of that moon next to Jupiter, see him three hundred and sixty times bigger than our one Moon appeareth to us: and as I believe that little moon to be much nearer to Jupiter than ours is; so his greatness must be by that considerably augmented; and they must constantly see that monstrous planet hanging over their heads, at a very small distance. And if it be true that the Gauls of old apprehended the falling of the heavens: the inhabitants of that moon have more reason to fear the falling of Jupiter.'

'It may be,' said she, 'they have that fright, instead of that of the eclipses, which you told me they are free from; and which must be supplied by some other piece of folly.'

'It must be so infallibly,' said I, 'Madam, for the great inventor of the third system of which I spoke to you the other day, the Tycho Brahe, one of the greatest astronomers that ever lived, was far from fearing eclipses as the vulgar do; but instead of that, he feared, if the first he met (as he went out of his house in the morning) were old, he instantly returned home, shut himself up, and did believe that day to be unlucky; nor would he dare to attempt business of the smallest consequence.'

'It is not just,' said the Marquise, 'that since that great man was not free from the fear of eclipses for nothing, that inhabitants of that little moon, should come off at an easier rate: let us give 'em no quarter, but force 'em to yield to some other folly. But since I will not trouble myself to guess at this time what that may be, pray solve me one difficulty, which my fancy has just now suggested; if the Earth be so little, in respect of Jupiter; do the inhabitants of Jupiter see our Earth? I am afraid we are altogether unknown to 'em.'

'Really, I believe it to be so,' said I, 'for the inhabitants of Jupiter must see the Earth ninety times less than Jupiter appears to us; which is too small to be perceived by them; and all we can imagine for our advantage, is to suppose that there are astronomers in Jupiter, who after having taken a great deal of pains and fitting excellent telescopes; and having chosen a very clear night for making the observation, they at last discovered in the heavens a little planet they had never seen before; and straight they set it down in their philosophical transactions of that country. The rest of the inhabitants of Jupiter, either never hear of it, or laugh at it if they do; the philosophers themselves whose opinion that discovery destroys, resolve not to believe it; and there are but some very rational people that will trouble themselves with the thoughts of it. These astronomers make new observations; they again look upon this little planet, and they begin to be assured that it is no fancy but a real thing; then they begin to conclude this little planet has a motion round the sun; and after a thousand observations, they at last find out that this motion, or revolution, is performed in a year's time. So that, thanks to these learned men, the inhabitants of Jupiter know our Earth is a planet and a world: the curious are earnest to look on it through a telescope; though 'tis so little 'tis hardly discoverable.'

'If it were not,' said the Marquise, 'very disagreeable for me to believe that our Earth is not to be perceived by the inhabitants of Jupiter, but by the help of a telescope, I should find an infinite pleasure in imagining, I should see those telescopes pointing towards us; and ours from a mutual curiosity are levelled at them, whilst those two planets gravely considering one another, the inhabitants of both ask at one and the same time, "What world is that?" "What people those?"'

'Don't go so fast, Madam,' said I; 'suppose the inhabitants of Jupiter could see our Earth; yet, they could never see us, or so much as suspect our Earth to be inhabited; or if anybody were fool enough to imagine it, God knows how he would be laughed at and ridiculed by the rest of the inhabitants. And it may be we are the cause that some philosophers in that world have been sued and persecuted for this opinion. However, I believe that the inhabitants of Jupiter are employed enough in the discovery of their own planet, without troubling themselves with the thoughts of us. And had Christopher Columbus been of that country, and understanding navigation so well, he could not have wanted employment.

'And the people of that world know not the hundredth part of its own inhabitants; whereas in Mercury (which is a very little planet) they are all neighbours one to another, and converse familiarly together; and they esteem it as but a walk to go round their little world; and if the inhabitants of Jupiter do not see us, you may easily judge, they can far less perceive Venus and Mercury, both which are more diminutive worlds, and further distant from it than we. But in lieu of this, they see Mars, and there are four moons, and Saturn with the five that belong to him. There are planets enough to perplex all the astronomers there: and nature has had the goodness to hide from 'em what remains of the universe.'

'What,' said the lady Marquise, 'do you look upon that as favour?'

'Without a doubt,' said I, 'Madam, there is in this great tourbillion or whirling of the Sun sixteen planets. And nature, who is willing to save us the labour of studying all their motions, has discovered to us only seven of them; and is not that a great favour. But we who are not sensible of that grace have so ordered the matter that by our endeavours we have found out the other nine, which nature had concealed from us, and we are sufficiently punished for it by the great pains and labour which is at present requisite for the study of astronomy.'

'I see,' answered she, 'by the number of sixteen planets, that Saturn must have five moons.'

'He has so,' said I, 'Madam, and two of the five are discovered very lately, but there is yet something more remarkable in that planet; for his year is as long as thirty of ours; and consequently there are climates in that world, where one night lasts for fifteen years together. Can you guess what nature has intended for the enlightening of night so long and dreadful? She was not satisfied to bestow on Saturn five moons; but has also given him a great circle or ring, which environs him entirely, and which is elevated sufficiently high enough to be out of the shadow of this planet. It reflects the light of the Sun perpetually upon the inhabitants of Saturn, who have the misfortune to live in that climate that is so long a time deprived of the influence of his beams.'

'Well,' said the Marquise (with the air of a person returned to herself from some great astonishment), 'all that you say is contrived with wonderful order, and sure nature has seen and provided for the necessity of some animate beings; and that the distribution of these moons was not a work of chance, since they are bestowed only upon these planets that are at a great distance from the Sun, the Earth, Jupiter and Saturn; for Venus and Mercury have no need on 'em; they enjoy but too much light already; and their nights are very short; and it may be the inhabitants of this planet esteem night a greater benefit of nature, than the day itself.'

'But hold,' said Madam the Marquise, 'it seems to me that Mars, who is further distant from the Sun than the Earth, ought to have a moon too.'

'I must confess,' said I, 'Madam, he has none; but certainly, the inhabitants of that planet enjoy some other advantage, which supplies that defect. You have seen several bodies, both liquid and dry, which draw in the light of the Sun; and afterwards shine and cast a light in the dark. It may be that there are great rocks very high; which are naturally of such a kind of substance as to receive great provision of light in the daytime from the Sun, which they restore to the night; and if it be so, you cannot deny, but it must be a very pleasant scene or representation, to see all those rocks from all quarters begin to shine, as soon as the Sun is down, and make magnificent illuminations without art or expense. You know also that in America there are certain birds which shine so in the dark that one may read by their light, as well as by that of a candle; and who knows, but there are many of these birds in the planet Mars, which fly around and enlighten that worlds as soon as the sun is set?'

'Your rocks and your shining birds,' said the Marquise, 'do not all satisfy me. I confess such objects would be very pretty; but since nature has given so many moons to Saturn and Jupiter 'tis a sign that they are absolutely necessary as well as to Mars. I should have been glad that all the worlds distant from the Sun could have had their moons; and that Mars might not have been so disagreeably excepted.'

'Oh! Madam,' said I, 'if you think it worth your pains to make any further progress in philosophy, you must accustom yourself to such exceptions; and in the best systems there are always some things that agree exactly; but there are other things that one must adjust as well as one can, or leave them as they are, if there be no hopes to overcome the difficulty. Let us do so if you please with Mars; and since he is not favourable to us, say no more of him. And tell me if it would not be strangely surprising if we were in the world of Saturn, to see above our heads in the night that great ring in the form of a semi-circle, going from opposite points of the horizon; and which reflecting the light of the Sun upon us, would have the effect of a continued moon.'

'And shall we place no inhabitants upon that great ring?' said the Marquise, laughing.

I answered her that (though in the humour I was in, I was inclined to put inhabitants everywhere) I confess, I dare not set any upon so irregular a habitation; but for the five little moons, there is no dispensing with them, for they must have inhabitants.

'But some do imagine that this ring or great circle is composed of moons joined very near together, having all an equal motion, and turning one way, and that the five little moons I spoke of had only escaped out of this great ring, what an infinity of worlds are there then in the tourbillion or whirlings of Saturn? And yet whatever is the cause, the inhabitants of Saturn are miserable enough, notwithstanding the assistance of this great ring. 'Tis true it give them light, but what kind of light? Sure a feeble one at that great distance from the Sun, where she herself appears to 'em but as a little pale star, a very faint heat and light, so that if you would carry some of the inhabitants of Saturn to our coldest countries, as Greenland or Lapland, you would see 'em all of a sweat and melt away with heat.'

'You give me an idea of Saturn,' said the Marquise, 'that makes me shiver with cold; whereas before you warmed me as much with the descriptions you gave me of Mercury.'

'There is a necessity,' said I, 'that the two worlds that are at the extremity of this great tourbillion, must be contrary one to another in every thing.'

'At that rate,' said she, 'the inhabitants of Saturn must be very wise; for you told me that the inhabitants of Mercury were downright mad.'

'If the people of Saturn,' said I, 'be not wise, they are at least in all appearance so, and are very phlegmatic, they know not what it is to laugh; and who take a whole day's time at least, to answer the most trifling question: they would have looked upon the grave Cato the Censor as too wild and youthful for their conversation.'

'There is a thought come into my head,' said the Marquise; 'all the inhabitants of Mercury are very lively, and the inhabitants of Saturn extremely dull: now upon our Earth we have a mixture of both, some are very airy and some as insipid: does not that proceed from our being situate in the middle, between these two worlds, that we participate so of the qualities of both these extremes; and there is no fixed settled character of mankind; some resemble the inhabitants of Mercury, others of Saturn; and we are a mixture of all the several kinds of people, that inhabit all the other planets?'

'I like that idea well enough,' said I, 'we are of such an extravagant composition, that one would really believe that we were collected and drawn together from all the other worlds. And at this rate, 'tis very convenient to live in ours, since here we see an abridgment of all that can be seen in the other worlds.'

'At least,' said the Marquise, 'our world has one real advantage and conveniency, that it is neither so hot as Mercury or Venus, nor so cold as Jupiter and Saturn: and we have the good luck, over and above, to be born in a climate of this Earth, that has neither excess of heat nor cold. And if a certain philosopher thanked nature for being a man and not a beast, a Greek, and not a Barbarian; for my part, I thank her, that I inhabit the most temperate climate of the planet.'

'If you will trust me,' said I, 'Madam, you ought to thank her for being young, and not old, young, handsome, and a French woman, and not a young handsome Italian. You have an abundance of other reasons of gratitude, than those of the situation of your tourbillion, or the temperate qualities of your country.'

'Good God,' said she, 'suffer me to be grateful for everything; even to the very tourbillion where I was born: the measure of the happiness bestowed upon us is too little to lose any part of it; and it is good to have such a sense and taste of the commonest and most inconsiderable things, as to turn all to our advantage and profit. If we should look after no other pleasure or satisfaction, than this world afforded, we should enjoy but very few, expect 'em long, and pay dear for 'em.'

'If philosophy be the pleasure you propose,' said I, 'Madam, I have the boldness to wish that when you remember the tourbillions, you would be pleased to think of me.'

'Yes,' answered she, 'provided you take care your philosopher furnishes me always with new pleasure.'

'At least, for tomorrow,' answered I, 'I hope you shall not want; for I have the fixed stars prepared for you, which surpass all you have hitherto heard.'

My lady Marquise was very impatient to know what should become of the fixed stars.

'Can they be inhabited as the planets are?' said she to me. 'Or are they not inhabited? What shall we make of 'em?'

'If you would take the pains, you could not fail to guess,' said I, 'Madam, the fixed stars cannot be less distant from the Earth, than fifty million leagues; nay, some astronomers make the distance yet greater; that between the Sun and the remotest planet is nothing if compared to the distance between the Sun or Earth, and the fixed stars; we do not trouble ourselves to number 'em, their lustre as you see is both clear and bright. If the fixed stars receive their light from the Sun, it must certainly be very weak and faint before it comes to 'em, having passed through a hundred and fifty millions of miles of the celestial substance, I spoke of before: then consider, the fixed stars are obliged to reflect this borrowed light upon us at the same distance, which in reason must make that light yet paler and more faint. It is impossible that this light, if it were borrowed from the Sun and not only suffered a reflection, but passed through twice the distance of a hundred and fifty millions of miles, could have that force and vivacity that we observe in the fixed stars. Therefore I conclude they are enlightened of themselves; and are by consequence so many suns.'

'Do not I deceive myself,' cried out the Marquise, 'do I see whither you are going to lead me? Are you not about to tell me the fixed stars are so many suns, and that our Sun is the centre of a great tourbillion which turns round him; what hinders but a fixed star may be the centre of a tourbillion, whirling or turning round it? Our Sun has planets, which he enlightens, why may not every fixed star have planets also?'

'I have nothing to answer but what Phaedra said to Oenone, 'tis you that have hit it.'

'But,' said she, 'I see the universe to be so vast, that I lose myself, I know not where I am, and have conceived nothing all this while. What is the universe thus divided into tourbillions, confusedly cast together? Is every fixed star the centre of a tourbillion; and it may be full as big as our space, wherein our sun and planets have their revolution, is nothing but an inconsiderable part of the universe? And that every fixed star must comprehend and govern an equal space with our Sun? This confounds, afflicts, and frightens me.'

'And for my part,' said I, 'it pleases and rejoices me; when I believed the universe to be nothing, but this great azure vault of the heaven, wherein the stars were placed, as it were so many golden nails or studs, the universe seems to me too little and straight; I fancied myself to be confined and oppressed. But now when I am persuaded that this azure vault has a greater depth and a vaster extent, and that 'tis divided into a thousand and a thousand different tourbillions or whirlings, I imagine I am at more liberty, and breath a freer air; and the universe appears to me to be infinitely more magnificent. Nature has spared nothing in her production, and hath profusely bestowed her treasures upon a glorious work worthy of her: you can represent nothing so august to yourself as this prodigious number of tourbillions, whose centre is possessed by a sun that makes the planets turn round him. The inhabitants of the planets of any of these infinite tourbillions see from all sides the enlightened centre of the tourbillion with which they are environed; but cannot discover the planets of another, who enjoy but a faint light, borrowed from their own sun, which it does not dart further than its own sphere of activity.'

'You show me,' said the Marquise, 'so vast a prospect that my sight cannot reach to the end of it: I see clearly the inhabitants of our world; and you have plainly presented to my reason the inhabitants of the Moon, and other planets of all the other tourbillions. I confess, they seem to me to be sunk into so boundless a depth, that whatever force I put upon my fancy, I cannot comprehend 'em; and indeed you have annihilated 'em by the expressions you made use of in speaking of 'em and their inhabitants. You must certainly call 'em the inhabitants of one of the planets, of one of these infinite tourbillions; and what shall become of us in the middle of so many worlds; since the title you give to the rest agrees to this of ours? And for my part, I see the Earth so dreadfully little, that hereafter I shall scorn to be concerned for any part of it. And I admire why mankind are so very fond of power, so earnest after grandeur, laying design upon design, circumventing, betraying, flattering, and poorly lying, and are at all this mighty pains to grasp a part of a world they neither know nor understand not anything of these mighty tourbillions. For me, I'll lazily condemn it, and my carelessness shall have this advantage by my knowledge that when anybody shall reproach me with my poverty, I will with vanity reply, "Oh! You do not know what the fixed stars are."'

'I do believe,' said I, 'Madam, that Alexander the Great himself did not know: for a certain author who holds that the Moon is inhabited says very gravely that it was impossible, but Aristotle must be of so reasonable an opinion (for how could such a truth escape so great a man as Aristotle?) but that he would never say anything of it for fear of displeasing Alexander, for had he known there had been a world which he could not have conquered, it would have reduced him to certain despair. There was yet more reason to conceal the tourbillions of the fixed stars from him; if they had been known in those days, he would have made his court very ill to that great prince, who should but have mentioned 'em. As for who knows 'em, I am very sorry I can draw no advantage from that knowledge, which can cure nothing but ambition and disquiet, and none of these diseases trouble me. I confess a kind of weakness in love, a kind of frailty for what is delicate and handsome, this is my distemper, wherein the tourbillions are not concerned at all. The infinite multitude of other worlds may render this little in your esteem, but they do not spoil fine eyes, a pretty mouth, or make the charms of wit ever the less. These will still have their true value, still bear a price in spite of all the worlds in the universe.'

'It is a strange thing,' said the Marquise laughing, 'that love saves himself from all dangers, and there is no system or opinion that can hurt him. But tell me frankly, are your systems certainly true? Do not dissemble, for I promise to keep it secret: I fancy 'tis founded upon a very small bottom, a fixed star enlightened of itself, as the Sun is, and therefore it must be a sun, the soul and centre of the world having planets turning round it as that also has.'

'Is this absolutely necessary?' says she.

'I fear, Madam,' said I, 'since we are always in the humour of mixing some little gallantries with our most serious discourses, give me leave to tell you that mathematical reasoning is in some things near akin to love; and you cannot allow the smallest favour to a lover, but he will soon persuade you to yield another, and after that a little more, and in the end prevails entirely; so if you grant the least principle to a mathematician, he will instantly draw a consequence from it, which you must yield also, and from that another, and then a third, and maugre all your resistance, in a short time, he will lead you so far that you cannot retreat. These two sorts of men, the lover and philosopher, always take more than is given 'em. You must acknowledge that when I see two objects alike in everything that I do see, I have reason to believe them to be also alike in what I see not; for where is the hindrance or difficulty? From thence I have argued that the Moon is inhabited because it is like the Earth; that the other planets are inhabited because they are like the Moon. I find that the fixed stars are like our Sun as to what I see; and therefore, I conclude that they are suns, and have planets turning round about 'em; and everything else we attribute to our suns. Now, Madam, you are too far engaged to retire; and therefore you must generously yield.'

'By this rule of resemblance,' said she, 'which you make betwixt our Sun and the fixed stars, the inhabitants of another tourbillion, must only see our Sun as a small fixed star, which only appears to them, during their night.'

'Without doubt,' said I, 'Madam, our Sun is so near us, in respect of the suns of the other tourbillions, that his light must have infinitely greater force upon our sight than the light of the other suns; when we see our Sun, we see nothing else, his brightness makes all other things disappear. In another great tourbillion, where another sun governs, he in his turn removes and darkens our Sun, which does not appear, but in the night as a fixed star amongst the other strange suns (that is) fixed stars, and our Sun appears to the inhabitants of that tourbillion in the great vault of heavens, as a star of some constellation, such as the bear or the bull. As to the planets which turn round him (as our Earth for example) since they cannot see it at so great a distance, they do not so much as think of it, so that all these suns are suns by day for the tourbillion which they govern, and fixed stars by night; for all the other, every one of them is the only one of his kind in his own worlds; but serve only to make up the number of fixed stars for all the other worlds.'

'Notwithstanding,' said she, 'of this equality of resemblance of the worlds, yet I cannot believe, but they differ in a thousand things, for likeness upon the main does not hinder infinite little differences.'

'Most certainly,' said I; 'but the difficulty will be to find out those differences. What do I know but in one tourbillion, there are more planets round it than in another? In one there are inferior planets turning round the greater, in another there are none at all. In one tourbillion the planets are gathered together, as it were a little party, round their sun, and beyond them a vast vacuity, extending to the next tourbillion; in another, the planets take their course towards the extremity of their tourbillion, and leave a void in the middle, and I do not doubt but there are tourbillions destitute of planets; and others, where the planets rise and fall in respect of their sun, according to the changes of counterpoise which balances 'em. What would you have, Madam? Have not I said enough for a man that was never out of his own tourbillion?'

'No,' said she, 'not for the quantity of worlds which you say there is. What you have described will suffice but for five or six, and I see thousands.'

'What would you say, Madam,' said I, 'if I should tell you that there are infinitely more fixed stars than those you see, that by the help of telescopes an unaccountable number are discovered, which we cannot see with our eyes alone; and that in one constellation, where we counted but twelve or fifteen stars, there have been discovered more than we see with our eye in the whole heavens?'

'I ask you pardon,' said she; 'I yield and confess, you have overcharged me with worlds and tourbillions.'

'Madam,' said I, 'I have still a reserve for you: you see that whiteness in the hemisphere, called the Milky Way; can you imagine what it is? 'Tis nothing but an infinity of little fixed stars, which cannot be seen by our eyes, because they are so very small, and are placed so near to one another, that they appear to be but one continued whiteness: I wish you could see this anthill of stars, and these seeds of worlds; they look like the Maldevia Islands, or those twelve thousand little isles, or banks of sand, separate only by small canals of the sea, which one may over-leap with as much ease as a ditch. So that these little tourbillions of the Milky Way, being so near one to another, may converse and shake hands with those of their neighbouring world; at least, the birds of one world may fly into another and they may teach pigeons to carry letters, as they do in the Levant. By which, the Sun, in his own tourbillion, as soon as he begins to spread his light, he faceth that of all other stranger-suns; for if you were in one of these little tourbillions of the Milky Way, your Sun would be so near to you; and by consequence, would have but little more power, force, or influence upon your eyes, than a hundred thousand other suns of the neighbouring tourbillions; you would then see your heaven shining with an infinite number of fires, very near to one another, and not far distant from you; and though you should lose the sight of your own Sun, you would still have light enough, and your nights would be no less bright than your days; at least, you would not be sensible of the difference; or, to speak more properly, you would have no night at all: the inhabitants of this world, accustomed to perpetual day, would be strangely surprised if one should tell 'em that there are several people in the universe who are under the tribulation of dismal, real nights, and who fall into long and profound darkness, and who, when the light returns, behold one and the same sun: they would look upon such people as the outcasts of nature, and the very thoughts of our sad condition would seize them with horror.'

'I do not ask you,' said the Marquise, 'whether there be any moons in the world of the Milky Way; I see very well, that they would be of no use to these planets that have no night; and who besides, move in too little room to be troubled with an equipage of inferior planets. But do you know that by your multiplying upon me such a multitude of worlds, you have started a great difficulty to my fancy, which, I doubt, you will hardly satisfy: the tourbillions, whose suns we see touch the tourbillions where we are, and all the tourbillions are round, how is it possible that so many different globes can touch one single one? This I would willingly understand, but find I cannot.'

'There's a great deal of sense,' said I, 'Madam, in your proposing of this difficulty, and no less in your not knowing how to salve it; for 'tis very judicious in itself, and unanswerable, as you understand it; and 'tis an argument of very little wit to answer an objection that is unanswerable. If our tourbillion were in the shape of a die, it would have six plain superficies, and would be very far from being round; yet upon every one of these six superficies, or flat sides, a tourbillion might be placed, being of the same figure: but instead of six flat sides, suppose it had twenty, fifty, or a thousand; then it were possible to place a thousand tourbillions upon it, every side bearing one; and you easily understand, that the more superficies, or flat sides any body has, the nearer it approaches to a globe: so a diamond cut in fossets on all sides, if those fossets were very small, that diamond would be as round almost as a pearl of the same bigness; the tourbillions are only round in this sense, they are composed of an infinite number of flat sides, and every one of 'em carries another tourbillion: the flat superficies are very unequal; here they are big, there they are little; the smallest superficies of our tourbillion, for example, answer to the Milky Way, and support all those little worlds; but if two tourbillions, that rest upon two neighbouring sides or faces, have any void space below between 'em (as that must fall out very often) nature, who will lose nothing and turns all her work to the best advantage, instantly fills up that vacuity with one, two, or it may be a thousand little tourbillions, which does not at all trouble or incommode the rest, and yet every one of these may have a world in it; so that there may be more worlds, than our tourbillion has flat sides to support. And I dare say, that although these little worlds were only made to fill up chinks in the universe, which otherwise would have been useless, and that they are altogether unknown to the other world which touch them; yet I doubt not but they are very well contented with their own condition, and 'tis they whose little suns we discover by the helps of telescopes, whose number is so prodigious. In fine, all these tourbillions are so rightly adjusted, and joined to one another in so delicate a form, that every one turns round his own sun, without changing his situation; every one takes that way of turning, which is most proper and commode to its place. They are fixed to one another like the wheels of a watch, assisting one another in their motions, and yet moving contrary to one another. And 'tis said, that every world is like a balloon, or football, which swells and fills of itself, and which would extend further, if it were not hindered by neighbouring worlds, who press it, and then it shrinks to its first form; after that it swells anew, and is again depressed. And the philosophers pretend that the fixed stars transmit to us a trembling light, and an unequal sparkling, because their tourbillions push against ours, and ours against theirs.'

'I am extremely in love,' said the Marquise, 'with these ideas you give me of the balloons, which swell and fall every moment; and those worlds, which are always jostling together: but, above all, I am pleased to consider that this strife amongst 'em produces a commerce of light, which is the only traffic they can have.'

'No, no,' said I, 'Madam; that is not the only traffic; the neighbouring worlds send envoys sometimes to us, and that with a great deal of splendour. We have comets from thence too, who are always adorned with shining hair, a venerable beard and a royal train.'

'Good God!' said the Marquise, laughing; 'what ambassadors are these? We could easily dispense with their visits, for they do nothing but fright us.'

'They fright only fools and children, Madam,' said I; 'but of those ignorant, I confess, there are a great number. The comets are nothing but planets which belong to some neighbouring tourbillion, who make their course toward the extremity, or outside of it: but this tourbillion being pressed by others that encompass it, 'tis rounder above than it is below, and it is from below that they appear to us. These planets which have begun to move in a circle above, and not foreseeing that their tourbillion will fail 'em below, because it is, as it were embarassed or squeezed in that part; these planets, which we call comets, are necessitated for the continuance of their circular motion to come into another tourbillion, which happens sometimes to be ours, making their passage through the extremity of it. They all appear to us highly elevated, their course being constantly above Saturn.

''Tis very necessary for the defence of our system (for reasons that do not at all relate to our present subject) that there should be a great vast space betwixt Saturn, and the extremities of our tourbillion, free from planets. Our adversaries do constantly reproach us with the unusefulness of this great void; but let 'em not trouble their heads with that, for we have found a use for it; and it is the apartment, or chambers of state, where we receive the stranger planetary ambassadors.'

'I understand you,' said she, 'and am pleased with your chamber of state; for we do not permit 'em to come directly in the middle of our tourbillion, but receive 'em as the grand seignior does his foreign ministers; he does 'em not the honour to lodge in Constantinople, but sends 'em to the suburbs.'

'Madam,' replied I, 'we agree with the Turks also in one more thing; that is (as they) so we receive ambassadors, but send none; for none of our planets ever go to visit other worlds.'

'At this rate,' said the Marquise, 'we are very proud, yet I know not what to think of the matter; these stranger-planets, with their long tails and beards, have usually but a scurvy threatening look, and it may be they are sent to terrify us; whereas ours, not being made of that terrible form, would not be so proper to frighten people, were they sent into another world.'

'These tails and beards,' said I, 'are not real, but only appearances, and these stranger-planets differ in nothing from ours; but entering into our tourbillion, they take a tail, or a beard from a certain kind of illumination which they receive from the Sun; which as yet, is not fully explained amongst us. But let this be found out when it can, we now are sure it is nothing but a kind of illumination, or false light.'

'I wish then,' said the Marquise, 'that our Saturn would take a tail, or a beard, and go into some other tourbillion to frighten its inhabitants; and that afterwards, laying aside this terrible equipage, he would return, with the rest of the planets, to his own place.'

'"Twill be better for him,' said I, 'not to go out of our tourbillion: I have told you already of the encounter between two tourbillions pushing against one another; and I believe, upon that occasion, a poor planet is strangely shaken, and that his inhabitants are not the better for it. We believe ourselves very miserable when we see a comet appear, but it is the comet itself that is most unhappy.'

'I do not believe that,' said the Marquise, 'for it brings inhabitants to us in good health; and you know, nothing is wholesomer than change of air; as for us that never go out of our own, life languishes but dully on. If the inhabitants of a comet had but the skill to foresee their passage into our world, those who have already made that voyage will tell these new adventurers what they will see in their way. "A planet", say they, "which has a great ring round him", meaning Saturn; and then you will see another that has four little ones following him, and it may be that amongst them there are people set apart on purpose for observing the very minute when they should enter into our world, and who are instantly to cry out, "A new sun! A new sun!" As our mariners do, "Land! Land!" after a long sea-voyage.'

'I hope you will no longer pity the inhabitants of a comet; but no doubt, you will commiserate those who live in a tourbillion where the sun comes to be extinct, and leaves them in eternal night.'

'What!' cried out Madam the Marquise, 'can suns be extinguished?'

'Yes,' said I, 'without dispute. The ancients have seen fixed stars in the firmament, which we see no more; these suns have lost their light: a great desolation certainly for that tourbillion, and a great mortality for all the inhabitants of its planets; for there is no living without a sun.'

'That idea,' said she, 'is too mournful; is there no way to pass it by?'

'If you please,' said I, 'Madam, I'll tell you what the very learned men say; that the fixed stars which have disappeared are not however extinguished, but that they are half-suns; that is to say, they have one side obscure, and the other enlightened; and as they turn upon their own axis, sometimes they present their enlightened half, and then we see 'em; and sometimes their obscure half, and then we lose 'em. To oblige you, Madam, I shall follow this opinion because 'tis more favourable than the other; but it must be only for certain stars, who have regular seasons of appearing and disappearing, as hath been discovered; otherwise these half-suns cannot subsist. But what shall we say of stars that disappear, and do not show themselves again after the time in which they ought certainly to have performed the revolution upon their own axis? You are too just, Madam, to oblige me to belie that there are stars and half-suns: however, for your satisfaction, I will endeavour to solve this objection another way. Those suns shall not be extinguished then, but shall only be sunk into the depth of the vast heavens, which removes 'em from our sight; and in that case, these suns are followed by their tourbillions, and all is well. 'Tis true that the greatest part of the fixed stars have no such motion as carry them from us; if they had, they might as well approach more near us, and we should see 'em sometimes bigger, sometimes less; which we can never fall out. Let us therefore suppose that there are some little tourbillions of less light and activity which slide in among the others, and make certain turnings; after which, they come back again, whilst in the meantime the great tourbillions remain where they did before; and 'tis a strange misfortune that there should be certain fixed stars which appear to us, and after a great deal of time of appearing and disappearing, entirely vanish, and are lost. In that time the half-suns that were sunk into the heavens would disappear once, and not to appear again for a long time. Resolve well what to think, Madam, and take courage; there is a necessity that these stars must be suns, which grown obscure enough to be invisible to our sight, are afterwards enlightened, and in the end must lie extinguished.'

'How,' said the Marquise; 'can a sun be obscured, or entirely extinguished, who is himself the fountain of light?'

'The most easily in the world,' said I, 'Madam: according to the opinion of Descartes our Sun has spots; let 'em be scum or vapours, or what else you will, these spots may condense, and many of 'em may come together, and form a kind of crust, which may afterwards augment, and then farewell the Sun and all its light. 'Tis said, we escaped once very hardly for the Sun was grown extremely pale for several years together; and particularly the year after the death of Julius Caesar, it was the crust that began to gather, and the force or heat of the Sun broke and dissipated it; but had it continued, we had been all undone.'

'You make me tremble,' said the Marquise; 'and not that I understand the consequences of the paleness of the Sun, I shall henceforth every morning, instead of going to my looking glass to consult my own face, go and look up to the heavens to consider that of the Sun.'

'Madam,' said I, 'be assured there goes a great deal of time to ruin a world.'

'Then,' said she, 'there is nothing requisite but time.'

'I acknowledge it, Madam,' said I; 'all this vast mass of matter which composes the universe is in perpetual motion, from which no part of it is entirely exempt; and therefore changes must come sooner or later, but always in time proportionable to the effect. The ancients were foolish to imagine that the celestial bodies were of an unchangeable nature, because they never saw any change in 'em; but they had neither leisure nor life long enough to undeceive themselves by experience; but the ancients were young in respect of us. Suppose now, Madam, that the roses, which last but for a day, should write histories and leave memorials from one to another; the first would have described the picture of their gardener of a certain manner; and after fifteen thousand ages of roses, the others that had followed 'em would have altered nothing in that description of the gardener, but would have said "We have always seen the same gardener, since the memory of the roses we have seen but him, he has always been as he is, he dies not as we do; nay, he changes not, and certainly will never be other than he is." Would this way of arguing of the roses be good? Yet it would be better grounded than that of the ancients, concerning celestial bodies; and though there had never happened any change in the heavens to this day, and though they should seem to last forever yet I would not believe it, but would wait for a longer experience; nor ought we to measure the duration of anything by that of our own scanty life. Suppose a thing had a being a hundred thousand times longer than ours, should we therefore conclude it should last for ever? Eternity is not so easy a matter; and some things must have passed many ages of men, one after another, before any sign of decay appeared in 'em.'

'I am not so unreasonable,' said the Marquise, 'as to consider the worlds as things eternal, nor will I do them the honour to compare 'em to your gardener, who lived for so many ages longer than the roses: they are themselves but as a rose, which are produced but in a garden, that bud one day, and fall the next; and as those roses die, new ones succeed; so for some ancient stars that disappear, other new ones are born in their places, and that defect in nature must be so repaired, and no species can totally perish. Some will tell you they are suns, which draw near to us after having been long lost in the depth of the heavens; others will say they are suns that have cast off the crust which began to cover them. I could easily believe all this, yet I should believe also that the universe was made in such a manner that new suns have been, and may be, formed in it from time to time; and what should hinder the substance proper to make suns from gathering together, and producing new worlds? And I am the more inclined to believe these new productions, since they are more correspondent to the great idea I have of the glorious works of nature. And why should not she who knows the secret to bring forth and destroy herbs, plants and flowers, in a continued succession, practise also the same secret on the worlds, since one costs her no more pains and expense than the other.'

'Indeed,' says the Marquise, 'I find the worlds, the heavens and the celestial bodies so subject to change that I am altogether returned to myself.'

'Let us return yet more,' said I, 'and if you please, make this subject no longer that of our discourse; besides you are arrived at the utmost bounds of heaven; and to tell you, that there are any stars beyond that, were to make myself a wiser man than I am, place worlds there, or place none there, it depends upon your will. These vast invisible regions are properly the empires of philosophers, which it may be are or are not, as they themselves shall fancy. 'Tis sufficient for me to have carried your understanding as far as your sight can penetrate.'

'What,' cried out the Marquise, 'have I the system of all the universe in my head, am I become so learned?'

'Yes, Madam, you know enough; and with this advantage, that you may believe all or nothing of what I have said, as you please. I only beg this as a recompense for my pains that you will never look on the heavens, Sun, moons or stars, without thinking about me.'

The general applause this little book of the plurality of worlds has met with, both in France and England in the original, made me attempt to translate it into English. The reputation of the author (who is the same, who writ the *Dialogues of the Dead*), the novelty of the subject in vulgar languages, and the authors introducing a woman as one of the speakers in these five discourses, were further motives for me to undertake this little work; I thought an English woman might adventure to translate anything a French woman may be supposed to have spoken. But when I had made a trial, I found the task not so easy as I believed at first. Therefore, before I say anything, either of the design of the author, or of the book itself, give me leave to say something of translation of the prose in general. As for translation of verse, nothing can be added to that incomparable essay of the late Earl of Roscommon, the nearer the idioms or turn of the phrase of two languages agree, 'tis the easier to translate one into the other. Italian, Spanish and French, are all three at best corruptions of Latin, with the mixture of Gothic, Arabic and Gaulish words. Italian, as it is nearest Latin, is also nearest English: for its mixture being composed of Latin, and the languages of the Goths, Vandals, and other northern nations, who overran the Roman Empire, and conquered its language with its provinces, most of these northern nations spoke Teutonic or dialects of it, of which English is one also; and that's the reason, that the English and Italian learn the language of one another sooner than any other; because not only the phrase, but the accent of both do very much agree, Spanish is next of kin to English, for almost the same reason. Because the Goths and Vandals, having overrun Africa, and kept possession of it for some hundred of years, where mixing with the Moors, no doubt, gave them a great tincture of their tongue. These Moors afterwards invaded and conquered Spain; besides Spain was before that also invaded and conquered by the Goths, who possessed it long after the time of the two sons of Theodosius the Great, Arcadius and Honorius. French, as it is most remote from Latin, so the phrase and accent differ most from English. It may be it is more agreeable with Welsh, which is near akin to the Basbritton and Biscagne languages, which is derived from the old Celtic tongue, the first that was spoken amongst the ancient Gauls, who descended from the Celts.

French therefore is of all the hardest to translate into English. For proof of this, there are other reasons also. And first, the nearer the genius and humour of two nations agree, the idioms of their speech are the nearer; and everybody knows there is more affinity between the English and Italian people, than the English and the French, as to their humours; and for that reason, and for what I have said before, it is very difficult to translate Spanish into French; and I believe hardly possible to translate French into Dutch. The second reason is the Italian language is the same now it was some hundred of years ago, so is Spanish, not only as to the phrase, but even as to the words and orthography; whereas the French language has suffered more changes this hundred years past, since Francis the First, than the fashions of their cloths and ribbons, in phrase, words and orthography. So that I am confident a French man a hundred years hence will no more understand an old edition of Froissart's *History*, than he will understand Arabic. I confess the French arms, money and intrigues have made their language very universal of late, for this they are to be commended: it is an accident, which they owe to the greatness of their king and their own industry; and it may fall out hereafter to be otherwise. A third reason is, as I said before, that French being a corruption of Latin, French authors take a liberty to borrow whatever word they want from Latin, without further ceremony, especially when they treat of science. This the English do not do, but at second hand from French. It is modish to ape the French in everything: therefore, we not only naturalise their words, but words they steal from other languages. I wish in this and several other things, we had a little more of the Italian and Spanish humour, and did not chop and change our language, as we do our cloths, at the pleasure of every French tailor.

In translating French into English, most people are very cautious and unwilling to print a French word at first out of a new book, till use has rendered it more familiar to us; and therefore it runs a little rough in English, to express one French word, by two or three of ours; and this much, as to the ease and difficulty of translating these languages in general; but as to French in particular, it has many advantages of English, as to the sound, as ours has of French, as to the signification; which is another argument of the different genius of the two nations. Almost all the relatives, articles, and pronouns in the French language end in vowels and are written with two or three letters. Many of their words begin with vowels; so, that when a word after a relative, pronoun or article ends with a vowel, and begins with another, they admit their beloved figure apostrophe and cut off the first vowel. This they do to shun an ill sound; and they go against all the rules of sense and grammar, rather than fail; as for example, speaking of a man's wife they say, 'son épouse'; whereas in grammar, it ought to be 'sa épouse'; but this would throw a French man into a fit of fever, to hear one say, by way of apostrophe 's'épouse', as this makes their language run smoother, so by this they express several words very shortly, as 'Qu'entend je?', in English, 'What do I hear?' In this example, three words have the sound but of one, for sound prevails with them in the beginning, middle and end. Secondly, their words generally end in vowels, or if they do not, they do not pronounce the consonant, for the most part, unless there are two together, or that the next word be as with a vowel. Thirdly, by the help of their relatives, they can shortly, and with ease resume a long proceeding sentence in two or three short words; these are the advantages of the French tongue, all which they borrow from the Latin. But as the French do not value a plain suit without a garniture, they are not satisfied with the advantages they have, but confound their own language with needless repetition and tautologies; and by a certain rhetorical figure, peculiar to themselves, employ twenty lines, to express what an English man would say, with more ease and sense, in five; and this is the great misfortune of translating French into English: if one endeavours to make it English standard, it is not translation. If one follows their flourishes and embroideries, it is worse than French tinsel. But these defects are only comparatively, in respect of English: and I do not say this so much, to condemn the French, as to praise our own mother-tongue, for what we think a deformity, they may think a perfection; as the Negroes of Guinea think us as ugly as we think them. But to return to my present translation.

I have endeavoured to give you the true meaning of the author, and have kept as near his words as possible; I was necessitated to add a little in some places, otherwise the book could not have been understood. I have used all along the Latin word axis, which is axle-tree in English, which I did not think so proper a word in a treatise of this nature; but 'tis what is generally understood by everybody. There is another word in the two last nights, which was very uneasy to me, and the more so for that it was so often repeated, which is tourbillion, which signifies commonly a whirlwind; but Monsieur Descartes understands it in a more general sense, and I call it a whirling; the author hath given a very good definition of it, and I need say no more, but that I retain the word unwillingly, in regard of what I have said in the beginning of this preface.

I know a character of the book will be expected from me, and I am obliged to give it to satisfy myself for being at the pains to translate it, but I wish with all my heart I could forbear it. For I have that value for the ingenious French author, that I am sorry I must write what some may understand to be a satire against him. The design of the author is to treat of this part of natural philosophy in a more familiar way than any other hath done, and to make everybody understand him: for his end, he introduceth a woman of quality as one of the speakers in these five discourses, whom he feigns never to have heard any of such thing as philosophy before. How well he hath performed his undertaking you will best judge when you have perused the book. But if you would know beforehand my thoughts, I must tell you freely he hath failed in his design; for endeavouring to render this part of natural philosophy familiar, he hath turned it into ridicule; he hath pushed his wild notions of the plurality of worlds to that height of extravagancy, that he most certainly will confound those readers who have not judgement and wit to distinguish between what is truly solid (or, at least, probable) and what is trifling and airy: and there is no less skill and understanding required in this, than in comprehending the whole subject he treats of. And for his Lady Marquise he makes her say a great many very silly things, though sometimes she makes observations so learned, that the greatest philosophers in Europe could make no better. His way of arguing is extremely fine, and his examples and comparisons are for the most part extraordinary, just, natural and lofty, if he had not concluded with that of a rose, which is very irregular. The whole book is very unequal; the first, fourth, and the beginning of the fifth discourses are incomparably the best. He ascribes all to nature, and says not a word of God Almighty, from the beginning to the end; so that one would almost take him to be a pagan. He endeavours chiefly two things; one is, that there are thousands of worlds inhabited by animals, besides our Earth, and hath urged this fancy too far: I shall not presume to defend his opinion, but one may make a very good use of many things he hath expressed very finely, in endeavouring to assist his wild fancy. For he gives a magnificent idea of the vastness of the universe and of the almighty and infinite power of the creator, to be comprehended by the meanest capacity. This he proves judiciously by the appearances and distances of the planets and fixed stars; and if he had let alone his learned men, philosophical translations and telescopes in the planet Jupiter, and his inhabitants not only there, but in all the fixed stars, and even in the Milky Way, and only stuck to the greatness of the universe, he had deserved much more praise.

The other thing he endeavours to defend and assert is the system of Copernicus. As to this, I cannot but take his part as far as a woman's reasoning can go. I shall not venture upon the astronomical part, but leave that to the mathematicians; but because I know that when this opinion of Copernicus (as to the motion of the Earth, and the Sun's being fixed in the centre of the universe, without any other motion, but upon his own axis) was first heard of in the world, those who neither understood the old system of Ptolemy, nor the new one of Copernicus, said that this new opinion was expressly contrary to the holy Scriptures, and therefore not to be embraced; nay, it was condemned as heretical upon the same account. After it had been examined by the best mathematicians in Europe, and that they found it answered all the phenomena and motions of the spheres and stars better than the system of Ptolemy; that it was plainer, and not so perplexing and confused as the old opinion; several of these learned men therefore embraced this; but those that held out, when they saw all arguments against Copernicus would not do, they had recourse to what I said before, that this system was expressly against the holy Scriptures. Amongst this number is the learned Father Tacquet, a Jesuit; who, I am told, has writ a large course of mathematics, and particularly of astronomy, which is deservedly much esteemed. In the end of this treatise, he cites several texts of Scripture; and particularly, the nineteenth psalm, and the Sun standing still at the command of Joshua. If I can make it appear, that this text of Scripture is, at least, as much for Copernicus as Ptolemy, I hope it will not be unacceptable to my readers. Therefore, with all due reverence and respect to the word of God, I hope I may be allowed to say that the design of the Bible was not to instruct mankind of astronomy, geometry or chronology, but in the law of God, to lead us to eternal life; and the spirit of God has been so condescending to our weakness, that through the whole Bible, when anything of that kind is mentioned, the expressions are always turned to fit our capacities and to fit the common acceptance or appearances of things to the vulgar. As to astronomy, I shall reserve that to the last, and shall begin with geometry; and though I could give many instances of all three, yet I shall give but one or two at most. The measure and dimensions of Solomon's molten brass sea in 1 Kings 7:23, the words are these:

And he made a molten sea, ten cubits from one brim to the other, and was round all about, and his height was five cubits, and a line of thirty cubits did compass it round about.

That is to say the diameter of this vessel was a third of its circumference. This is indeed commonly understood to be so, but is far from a geometrical exactness, and will not hold to a mathematical demonstration, as to the just proportion between diameter and circumference of a circle. In the next place, as to chronology, I could give many instances out of the Bible, but shall only name two that are very apparent, and easy to be understood by the meanest capacity. See 1 Kings 6:1, the words are these:

And it came to pass, in the four hundred, and fourscore year after the children of Israel were come out of the land of Egypt, in the fourth year of Solomon's reign over Israel, in the month Zif, which is the second month, he began to build the house of the lord.

Compare this text and number of years with Acts 13 which is the beginning of St Paul's sermon to the Jews of Antioch, and the number of years therein contained. The words are these:

Verse 17. The God of this people of Israel chose our fathers, and exalted the people when they dwelt as strangers in the land of Egypt, and with an high hand brought he them out of it.

Verse 18. And about the time of forty years suffered he their manners in the wilderness.

Verse 19. And when he had destroyed seven nations in the land of Canaan, he divided their land to them by lot.

Verse 20. And after that, he gave unto them judges, about the space of four hundred and fifty years, until Samuel the prophet.

Verse 21. And afterwards they desired a king, and God gave them Saul, the Son of Kish, a man of the tribe of Benjamin, for the space of forty years.

Verse 22. And when he had removed him, he raised up unto them David to be their king.

King David the prophet reigned seven years in Hebron, and thirty-three years in Jerusalem; and for this see 1 Kings 2:11. To this you must add the first three years of his son Solomon, according to the text I have cited, in 1 Kings 6:1. Put all these numbers together, which are contained in St Paul's sermon at Antioch, with the reign of King David, the first three years of Solomon, and seven years of Joshua's government, before the land was divided by lot, which is expressly set down in Acts 13:19, the number of years will run thus: forty years in the wilderness, the seven years of Joshua, before the dividing the land by lot; from thence, till Samuel, 450 years; forty years for the reign of Saul, forty years for the reign of David, and the first three years of Solomon; all these numbers added together, make 580 years; which computation differs 100 years from that in Kings 6:1 which is but 480. It is not my present business to reconcile this difference; but I can easily do it; if anybody think it worth their pains to quarrel my boldness, I am able to defend myself.

The second instance is, as to the reign of King Solomon; for this, see 1 Kings 11:42, where it is said he reigned but forty years over Israel. Josephus says expressly, in the third chapter of his eighth Book of Antiquities, that King Solomon reigned eighty years, and died at the age of ninety-four. I would not presume to name this famous historian in contradiction to the holy Scriptures, if it were not easy to prove by the Scriptures, that Solomon reigned almost twice forty years. The Greek version of the Bible, called commonly the Septuagint, or seventy-two interpreters, has it most expressly in 3 Kings 2. But the first Book of Kings according to our translation in English says that Solomon sat upon the throne of his father David, when he was twelve years of age, but for confirmation, be pleased to see 1 Chronicles 22:5 and 29:1 where it is said, that Solomon was but young and tender for so great a work, as the building of the temple. Rehoboam, the son of Solomon, was forty-one years old when he began to reign, see 1 Kings 14:21. How was it possible then that Solomon could beget a son when he was but a child himself, or of eleven years of age according to the Septuagint? This difficulty did strangely surprise a primitive bishop, by name Vitalis, who proposed this doubt to St Jerome, who was strangely put to it to return an answer; and the learned holy father is forced at last to say, that the letter of the Scripture does often kill, but the spirit enlivens. The difficulty is still greater than what Vitalis proposed to St Jerome in his epistle. Rehoboam was the son of Naamah, an Ammonite, stranger woman, as you may see in 1 Kings 14:31. Now it is clear that Solomon did not abandon the law of God, nor give himself to strange women till the end of his reign, see 1 Kings 9 where he has so many strange wives and concubines, besides his lawful queen, the King of Egypt's daughter; and I hope this will convince any rational man, that the Scriptures name only the first forty years of the reign of King Solomon, which was the time wherein he did what was right in the sight of the Lord; which I think is demonstration, that the holy Scripture was not designed to teach mankind geometry, or instruct them in chronology.

The learned Anthony Godeau, Lord and Bishop of Venice, seems to have been sensible of this great difficulty; for in his learned Church-History, his epitome from Adam to Jesus Christ, writing the life of Solomon, he says he was twenty-three years old when he began his reign. Upon what grounds, or from what authority I know not; but this agrees better with the age of Solomon's son Rehoboam; but it doth not remove the difficulty, so well as what I have said.

I come now in the last place to perform what I undertook, which is to prove that the Scripture was not designed to teach us astronomy, no more than geometry or chronology. And to make it appear that the two texts cited by Father Tacquet, viz. that of 1 Sal. and Joshua 10:12, etc. are at least as much for Copernicus his system, as they are for Ptolemy's. The words of the 19th psalm are:

In them hath he set a tabernacle for the sun, which is as a bridegroom coming out of his chamber; and rejoices as a strong man to run his race etc.

That these words are allegorical is most plain. Does not the word 'set' import stability, fixedness and rest, as much as the words 'runs his race', and 'come forth of his chamber', do signify motion or turning round? Do not the words 'tabernacle' and 'chamber' express places of rest and stability? And why may not I safely believe, that this makes for the opinion of Copernicus, as well as for that of Ptolemy? For the words of the

Scriptures favour one opinion as much as the other. The texts of the suns standing still at the command of Joshua, are yet plainer for Copernicus, in Joshua 10 and the latter part of Verse 12, the words are these: 'Sun stand thou still on Gibeon, and thou Moon on the valley of Ajalon, etc.'

The best edition of the English Bible, which is printed in a small folio by Buck, in Cambridge, has an asterisk at the word 'stand', and renders it in the margin, from the Hebrew, 'Be thou silent.' If it be so in the Hebrew, 'be thou silent' makes as much for the motion of the Earth, according to Copernicus, as for the motion of the Sun according to Ptolemy, but not to criticise upon words, consider this miraculous passage; not only the Sun is commanded to stand still, but the Moon also, 'And thou Moon on the valley of Ajalon'. The reason the Sun was commanded to stand still was to the end the children of Israel might have light to guide them, to destroy their enemies. Now when by this miracle they had the light of the Sun, of what advantage could the Moon be to them? Why was she commanded to stand still upon the valley of Ajalon? Besides, be pleased to consider, the Holy Land is but a very little country or province: the valley of Ajalon is very near Gibeon, where Joshua spoke to both Sun and Moon together to stand still above, in places so near each other, it is demonstration that the Moon was at that time very near the Sun; and by consequence was at that time either a day or two before her change, or a day or two at most after new Moon; and then she is nearer to the body of the Sun, as to appearance, so could not assist the children of Israel with light, having so little of her own. It was then for some other reason that the Moon stood still; and for some other reason that it is taken notice of in holy Scripture. Both systems agree that the Moon is the nearest planet to the Earth and subservient to it, to enlighten it, during the night, in absence of the Sun. Besides this, the Moon has other strange effects, not only on the Earth itself, but upon all the living creatures that inhabit it; many of them are invisible, and as yet unknown to mankind; some of them are most apparent; and above all, her wonderful influence over the ebbing and flowing of the sea, at such regular times and seasons, if not interrupted by the accident of some storm, or great wind. We know of no relation or corresponding between the Sun and the Moon, unless it be what is common with all the rest of the planets, that the Moon receives her light from the Sun, which she restores again by reflection. If the Sun did move, according to the system of Ptolemy, where was the necessity of the Moon's standing still? For if the Moon had gone on her course, where was the loss or disorder in nature? She having, as I demonstrated before, so little light, being so very near her change, would have recovered her loss at the next appearance of the Sun, and the Earth could have suffered nothing by the accident; whereas the Earth moving at the same time, in an annual and diurnal course, according to the system of Copernicus, would have occasioned such a disorder and confusion in nature, that nothing less than two or three new miracles, all as great as the first, could have set the world in order again. The regular ebbings and flowings of the sea must have been interrupted, as also the appearing of the Sun in the horizon, besides many other inconveniences in nature; as, the eclipses of the Sun and Moon, which are now so regular, that an astronomer could tell you to a minute what eclipses will be for thousands of years to come, both of Sun and Moon; when, and in what climates they will be visible, and how long they will last, how many degrees and digits of those two great luminaries will be obscured. So that I doubt not but when this stupendous miracle was performed by the almighty and infinite power of God, his omnipotent arm did in an instant stop the course of nature, and the whole frame of the universe was at stand, though the Sun and Moon be only named, being, to vulgar appearance, the two great luminaries that govern the universe. This was the space of a day in time, yet can be called no part of time, since time and nature are always in motion, and this day was a stop of that course. What is there in all this wonderful stop of time that is not as strong for the system of Copernicus, as for that of Ptolemy? And why does my belief |of the motion of the Earth, and the rest of the Sun contradict the holy Scriptures? Am not I as much obliged to believe that the Sun lodges in a tabernacle? (as in Psalm 19). Are not all these allegorical sayings? In the above named edition of the English Bible of Buck's at Cambridge, see Isaiah 8:38 where the shadow returned ten degrees backwards, as a sign of King Hezekiah's recovery, and there follow these words: 'And the Sun returned ten degrees'; but on the margin you will find it from the Hebrew: 'The shadow returned ten degrees by the Sun'; and this is yet as much for Copernicus as Ptolemy. Whether God Almighty added ten degrees or hours to that day, or by another kind of miracle made the shadow to return upon the dial of Ahaz, I will not presume to determine; but still you see the Hebrew is most agreeable to the new system of Copernicus.

Thus I hope I have performed my undertaking, in making it appear, that the holy Scriptures, in things that are not material to the salvation of mankind, do altogether condescend to the vulgar capacity; and that these two texts (of Psalm 19 and Joshua 10) are as much for Copernicus as against him. I hope none will think my undertaking too bold, in making so much use of the Scriptures, on such an occasion. I have a precedent, much esteemed by all ingenious men; that is, Mr Burnet's *Book of Paradise and Antedeluvian World*, which encroaches as much, if not more on the holy Scriptures. But I have another reason for saying so much of the Scriptures at this time: we live in an age, wherein many believe nothing contained in that holy book, others turn it into ridicule: some use it only for mischief, and as a foundation and ground for rebellion. Some keep close to the literal sense, and others give the word of God only that meaning and sense that pleases their own humours, or suits best their present purpose and interest. As I quoted an epistle of St Jerome to Vitalis before, where that great father says, that the letter kills, but the Spirit enlivens; I think it is the duty of all good Christians to acquiesce in the opinion and decrees of the church of Christ, in whom dwells the spirit of God, which enlightens us to matters of religion and faith; and as to other things contained in the holy Scriptures relating to astronomy, geometry, chronology, or other liberal sciences, we leave those points to the opinion of the learned, who by comparing the several copies, translations, versions, and editions of the Bible, are best able to reconcile any apparent differences; and this with all submission to the canons of general councils and decrees of the church. For the school-men agitate and debate many things of higher nature, than the standing still or other motion of the Sun or the Earth. And therefore, I hope my readers will be so just as to think I intend no reflection on religion by this essay; which being no matter of faith, is free for everyone to believe, or not believe, as they please. I have adventured to say nothing, but from good authority: and as this is approved of by the world, I may hereafter venture to publish somewhat may be more useful to the public. I shall conclude therefore with some few lines, as to my present translation.

I have laid the scene at Paris, where the original was writ; and have translated the book near the words of the author.

I have made bold to correct a fault of the French copy, as to the height of our air or sphere of activity of the Earth, which the French copy makes twenty or thirty leagues, I call it two or three, because sure this was a fault of the printer, and not a mistake of the author. For Monsieur Descartes, and Monsieur Rohalt, both assert it to be but two or three leagues. I thought Paris and Saint-Denis having several steeples and walls, is more like Paris, than Greenwich is to London. Greenwich has no walls, and but one very low steeple, not to be seen from the Monument without a prospective glass. And I resolved either to give you the French book into English, or to give you the subject quite changed and made my own; but having neither health nor leisure for the last I offer you the first such as it is.

I find myself reduced almost to the same condition in which Cicero was when he undertook to put matters of philosophy into Latin; which, till that time, had never been treated of but in Greek. He tells us, it would be said, his works would be unprofitable, since those who loved philosophy, having already taken the pains to find it in the Greek, would neglect, after that, to read it again in Latin (that being the original); and that those who did not care for philosophy would not seek it, either in Latin or Greek. But to this Cicero himself answers; and says that those who were not philosophers would be tempted to the reading of it, by the facility they would find in its being in the Latin tongue; and that those who were philosophers would be curious enough to see how well it had been turned from Greek to Latin.

Cicero has reason to answer in this manner; the excellency of his genius, and the great reputation he had already acquired sufficiently defend this new undertaking of his, which he had dedicated to the benefit of the public. For my part, I am far from offering at any defence for this of mine, though the enterprise be the same; for I would treat of philosophy in a manner altogether unphilosophical, and have endeavoured to bring it to a point not too rough and harsh for the capacity of the numbers, nor too light and trivial for the learned. But if they should say to me, as they did to Cicero, that this work is not at all proper for the learned, nor would it instruct the rest of the world, who are careless of knowledge; far be it from me to answer as Cicero did, who, perhaps, in searching for a middle way to philosophy, such as would improve every understanding, I have taken that which possibly will be advantageous to none: it is very hard to keep to a medium, and

I believe I shall fierce take the pains to search a second method to please. And if it happen that this book should be read, I advertise those that have some knowledge in philosophy, that I have not pretended to instruct, but to divert them, in pretending to them in a more agreeable manner, that which they already know solidly; and I also advertise those to whom this subject is new that I believe it will at once instruct and please them. The knowing will act contrary to my intentions, if they seek only pleasure.

I will not amuse myself in telling you that I have taken out of philosophy the matter the most capable of inspiring a curiosity; for in my opinion, we ought to seek no greater interest than to know how this world which we inhabit is made, and that there are other worlds that resemble it, and that are inhabited as well as this. After all, I let those that please give themselves the trouble of finding out this truth, but I am sure they will not do it in compliance to my book. Those that have any thoughts to lose, may cast them away here: but all people are not in a condition, you will say, to make such an unprofitable experience of time.

In this discourse I have introduced a fair lady to be instructed in philosophy, which, till now, never heard any speak of it; imagining, by this fiction, I shall render my work more agreeable, and to encourage the fair sex (who lose so much time at their toilettes in a less charming study) by the example of a lady who had no supernatural character, and who never goes beyond the bounds of a person who has no tincture of learning, and yet understands all that is told her, and retains all the notions of tourbillions and worlds, without confusion. And why should this imaginary lady have the predecency of all the rest of her delicate sex? Or do they believe they are not as capable of conceiving that which she learned with so much facility?

The truth is Madam the Marquise applies herself to this knowledge; but what is this application? It is not to penetrate by force of meditation, into a thing that is obscure in itself or anything that is obscurely explained; 'tis only to read, and to represent to yourselves at the same time what you read, and to form some image of it that may be clear and free from perplexing difficulties. I ask of the ladies (for this system) but the same attention that they must give the *Princess of Clèves*, if they would follow the intrigue, and find out the beauties of it; the truth is, that the ideas of this book are not so familiar to the most part of ladies, as those of the *Princess of Clèves*; but they are not more obscure than those of the novel, and yet they need not think above twice at most, and they will be capable of taking a true measure, and having a just sense of the whole.

I do not pretend to take a system in the air, without a foundation, but I have made use of true philosophical reasons; and of those, employed as many as are necessary; and, as it happily falls out, the notions of philosophy upon this subject are pleasant; and at the same time that they satisfy the reason, they content the imagination with a prophet as agreeable, as if they had been made on purpose to entertain it.

Where I found some pieces not altogether so diverting as I wished, I gave them foreign ornaments: Virgil made use of the same method in his *Georgics*, where he adorned his subject (of itself altogether dull) with several digressions, and very often agreeably. Ovid himself has done as much in his *Art of Loving*, though the foundation of his theme was infinitely more agreeable than anything that could be mixed with it; therefore it is to be supposed he imagined it would be tiresome always to treat of one and the same thing, though it was of gallantry. But for my part, I, who have much more need of the assistance of digression, have, notwithstanding, made use of them very frugally: I have authorised them by the liberty of natural conversation, and have put them but in those places where I thought everybody would be glad to find them; I have put the greatest part of them in the beginning of my work, because the mind will not be then so well accustomed to the principal ideas that I present. In fine, I have taken them from the subject itself, or, at least, approaching to it.

I would not have any imagination of the inhabitants of the worlds that are entirely fabulous, but have endeavoured to relate only that which might be thought most reasonable; and the visions themselves that I have added, have something of a real foundation in them; the true and the false are here mixed, but they always are very easy to be distinguished; yet I do not undertake to justify a composure so fantastical: this is the most important point of this work, and 'tis this only that I cannot give a reason for; the public censure will inform me, what I ought to think of this design.

There remains no more for me to say in this Preface, but to speak to one sort of people, who, perhaps, will be most difficult to content (and yet I have very good reasons to give them, but, possibly, such as they will not take for current pay, unless they appear to them to be good); and these are the scrupulous persons who may imagine that in regard of religion there may be danger in placing inhabitants anywhere but on this Earth; but I have had a respect, even to the most delicate niceties of religion, and would not be guilty of anything that should shock it in a public work, though that care were contrary to my opinion. But that which will surprise you is that religion is not at all concerned in this system, where I fill an infinite number of worlds with inhabitants; and you need only reform and clear one error of the imagination. But when I shall tell you the Moon is inhabited, you presently represent to your fancy men made as we are; and if you are a little of the theologician, you will then be presently full of difficulties: the posterity of Adam could not possibly extend to the Moon, nor send colonies into that country; then they are not the sons of Adam, and that would be a great perplexing point in theology, to imagine there should be men, and those not to descend from Adam. There is no need of saying any more, all the difficulties are reduced to that, and the arguments we ought to employ in a tedious explanation, are too worthy of gravity to be put into this book, though perhaps I could answer solidly enough to their objections, if I undertook it; but 'tis certain, I have no need of answering them; let the men in the Moon do it, who are only concerned; for 'tis they that put the men there, I only put inhabitants, which, perhaps, are not men. What are they then? 'Tis not that I have seen them, that I speak of them; yet do not imagine that I design (by saying there are no men in the Moon) to evade your objections, but you shall see that 'tis impossible (according to the ideas that I have of the infinite diversity that nature ought to use in her works) that there can be none. This idea governs all the book, and it cannot be confuted by any philosopher; therefore I believe I shall meet with no objection from any, but those who speak of these entertainments, without having read them. But is this reason enough for me to depend on? No, 'tis rather a sufficient reason for me to fear this objection will be often urged in several places.

Bernard de Fontenelle was born in Rouen in 1657. Educated at a Jesuit college, he originally trained as a lawyer but gave up after only one case. He became interested instead in philosophy and in particular defending Cartesian theories. He began his writing career as a poet, subsequently turning his hand to a couple of operas which were received with limited success. De Fontenelle made his name with his *Lettres gallantes du chevalier d'Her*, a collection of letters describing society life. He followed this success with examinations of religious and philosophical matters and his *Entretiens sur la pluralité des mondes* was published in 1686. He was admitted to the French Academy in 1691 and was Secretary to the Academy of Sciences for more than forty years. His work was renowned for its novel-like style and for its ability to render philosophical and scientific ideas accessible to the average reader. He died in Paris, one month short of his hundredth birthday.

Aphra Behn was one of the first English professional women writers. She was born in Kent in 1640. In 1663 a visit to Venezuela and subsequent encounters there inspired her to write *Oroonoko*, a novel which was instrumental in radically changing the British attitude towards slavery. In 1666, Behn became attached to the Court and eventually was recruited as Charles II's spy and sent to work in Amsterdam. Following a spell in debtors' prison, Behn resolved to take up writing as an occupation; producing novels, poems and plays. She died in 1689 and was buried in Westminster Abbey.

HESPERUS PRESS

Hesperus Press is committed to bringing near what is far – far both in space and time. Works written by the greatest authors, and unjustly neglected or simply little known in the English-speaking world, are made accessible through new translations and a completely fresh editorial approach. Through these classic works, the reader is introduced to the greatest writers from all times and all cultures.

For more information on Hesperus Press, please visit our website: **www.hesperuspress.com**

SELECTED TITLES FROM HESPERUS PRESS

Author	Title	Foreword writer
Pietro Aretino	*The School of Whoredom*	Paul Bailey
Pietro Aretino	*The Secret Life of Nuns*	
Jane Austen	*Lesley Castle*	Zoë Heller
Jane Austen	*Love and Friendship*	Fay Weldon
Honoré de Balzac	*Colonel Chabert*	A.N. Wilson
Charles Baudelaire	*On Wine and Hashish*	Margaret Drabble
Giovanni Boccaccio	*Life of Dante*	A.N. Wilson
Charlotte Brontë	*The Spell*	
Emily Brontë	*Poems of Solitude*	Helen Dunmore
Mikhail Bulgakov	*Fatal Eggs*	Doris Lessing
Mikhail Bulgakov	*The Heart of a Dog*	A.S. Byatt
Giacomo Casanova	*The Duel*	Tim Parks
Miguel de Cervantes	*The Dialogue of the Dogs*	Ben Okri
Geoffrey Chaucer	*The Parliament of Birds*	
Anton Chekhov	*The Story of a Nobody*	Louis de Bernières
Anton Chekhov	*Three Years*	William Fiennes
Wilkie Collins	*The Frozen Deep*	
Joseph Conrad	*Heart of Darkness*	A.N. Wilson
Joseph Conrad	*The Return*	Colm Tóibín
Gabriele D'Annunzio	*The Book of the Virgins*	Tim Parks
Dante Alighieri	*The Divine Comedy: Inferno*	
Dante Alighieri	*New Life*	Louis de Bernières
Daniel Defoe	*The King of Pirates*	Peter Ackroyd
Marquis de Sade	*Incest*	Janet Street-Porter
Charles Dickens	*The Haunted House*	Peter Ackroyd
Charles Dickens	*A House to Let*	
Fyodor Dostoevsky	*The Double*	Jeremy Dyson
Fyodor Dostoevsky	*Poor People*	Charlotte Hobson
Alexandre Dumas	*One Thousand and One Ghosts*	